Acclaim for MOONLIGHT AND MISTLETOE!

"MOONLIGHT AND MISTLETOE is a charming mixture of madness, mayhem and pure magic! This funny, fast-paced Yuletide tale will leave you feeling warm and wonderful and believing there really is a Santa Claus. Delightful!"

—Nan Ryan, bestselling author of
A Lifetime of Heaven

"Maggie Davis' MOONLIGHT AND MISTLETOE is a wonderful Christmas romp, a delightfully comic view of small-town America, Southern-style. There's a harried sheriff, a spirited heroine, and a whole flock of fascinating secondary characters. The ending is the wildest, wackiest and most hilarious one I have ever come across. I absolutely loved this book!"

—Linda Lael Miller, *New York Times*
bestselling romance author

"MOONLIGHT AND MISTLETOE is an enchanting Cinderella tale guaranteed to put you in the most delightful Christmas spirit."

—Raine Cantrell, author of *Calico*

Books by Maggie Davis

Writing as Maggie Davis:
EAGLES
ROMMEL'S GOLD
THE SHEIK
THE FAR SIDE OF HOME
THE WINTER SERPENT
FORBIDDEN OBJECTS
SATIN DOLL
SATIN DREAMS
WILD MIDNIGHT
MIAMI MIDNIGHT
HUSTLE, SWEET LOVE
DIAMONDS AND PEARLS
TROPIC OF LOVE
DREAMBOAT

Writing as Katherine Deauxville:
DAGGERS OF GOLD
BLOOD RED ROSES

Writing as Maggie Daniels:
A CHRISTMAS ROMANCE
MOONLIGHT AND MISTLETOE

MOONLIGHT AND MISTLETOE

MAGGIE DANIELS

ST. MARTIN'S PAPERBACKS

MOONLIGHT AND MISTLETOE

Copyright © 1993 by Maggie Davis.

ISBN: 0-312-95147-7

Printed in the United States of America

St. Martin's Paperbacks edition / November 1993

10   9   8   7   6   5   4   3   2   1

For Janine Coughlin

with special thanks to
Detective Sergeant David A. Harrington
for info on picking locks and hot-wiring cars

Scarlett's Good Luck *Hoppin' John* Southern Heirloom Recipe for New Year's

Take one pound of dried black-eyed peas and soak overnight in large boiler.

Next day add smoked ham hock, salt, and black pepper to taste. Simmer until very tender.

Pour over helping of cooked rice. Serve with side garnish of chopped sweet onion, ketchup, and Tabasco sauce to taste.

Guaranteed to bring good luck if you've got your mouth full when the New Year comes in. At least in the South.

One

"TURN DOWN THOSE CHRISTMAS CAROLS," Sheriff Buck Grissom shouted. "Confound it, this is supposed to be a jail!"

As the recorded strains of "Deck the Halls" faded away under the invisible hand of a deputy in the jail's office, he turned back to the county social worker. "Am I glad to see you, Susan," he said fervently. "I need some help."

Susan Huddleston looked at Sheriff Grissom's six-feet-four-inch, Marine-trained body in its crisp black and tan uniform, thinking she'd hardly ever heard the sheriff admit he needed anyone's help. In their now-past relationship this had been one of their great problems: Buck was as stiff-necked as they came, even as a lover.

Behind the sheriff hung the brass-framed, life-sized portrait of Buck's father, Sheriff William Rutherford Grissom, Sr. The elder Grissom had been big and handsome, too. That is, if you liked steely blue eyes, mahogany-red hair, and a jaw that looked as if it were carved from native north Georgia granite.

"It must be something big," Susan said, choosing her words carefully. "I've never seen you this—ah, concerned."

"Concerned?" He gave her a distracted look as he opened the door to the women's part of the jail. "The way I feel I could cancel this damned Christmas altogether. I wish I had taken up my deputies' offer of that expense-paid fishing trip to Florida, to go with that rod and reel they gave me on my birthday."

Susan fought down a sudden desire to smile. The Jackson County sheriff's department wanted Buck to have his long-delayed vacation. Christmas in the mountains was usually a crime-free, quiet time—perfect, the department thought, for a Florida deep-sea fishing trip.

It wasn't that Buck's staff didn't love him, they just needed him out of their hair for a while. Anyone who had to live with the late William Grissom, Sr.'s, hard-driving, sometimes unbearably perfectionist son needed some time off occasionally. But Buck had turned down what his deputies had considered a foolproof offer. His staff was getting a little desperate.

Now he held the door to the cell block open. "Nothing's going right," he growled in Susan's ear. "For one thing, I've got that court injunction prohibiting the living manger scene from being shown in front of the courthouse, just served today. That manger scene's an institution, Susan, it's been dis-

2

played since nineteen fifty-two. People around here just don't understand what's happened."

Susan looked around the cell block, never crowded at any time but now, at the Christmas holidays, virtually deserted. "Buck, the issue is separation of church and state," she reminded him. "And the courthouse lawn *is* government property."

He turned to glower at her. "Dammit, Susan—Christmas has nothing to do with civil rights!"

She didn't blink. "This time it does."

"Now you sound like those parasite lawyers." He led the way through the men's part of the jail, empty except for one lone form sleeping in the drunk tank. "Christmas," Sheriff Buck said firmly, "is a time to bring folks together, not split them apart, and everybody's fighting over this thing. I've had the whole of Jackson County all over me—telephoning, dogging me at home, wanting to know why I can't do something about getting Mary and Joseph and Sally Holborn's youngest that was voted Best Child to Play the Infant Jesus back in front of the courthouse in time for Christmas shopping."

Buck, hearing earsplitting screams, stopped so quickly Susan nearly ran into him. Just beyond the open door they saw a county deputy, Moses Holt, dragging a violently resisting female over the plastic tile floor. They couldn't see her face as she half slithered, half bounced along since it was hidden by a gypsylike mop of black hair. But a hiked-up skirt revealed two long, shapely if dirty bare legs, and a bottom covered with gray-pink underwear panties. The air was blue with language that Jackson

County, still a stronghold of old-fashioned values, seldom heard from female lips.

"Whew," Susan murmured.

"Mose, we can't have this going on." The sheriff had to raise his voice to be heard over a colorful description of what Deputy Holt could do with his future existence. "Where's Mrs. Graham?" The matron handled the prisoners on the women's side of the jail.

Deputy Holt didn't have time to answer. "Don't just stand there, Sheriff, come help me," he panted as the prisoner's free arm snaked out and wrapped around a bar. "She grabbed hold of the desk while I was trying to fingerprint her, and it took me near forever to get her loose."

The girl suddenly swung her head close to the deputy's ankle. Moses Holt jerked his leg away just in time.

"That's our problem right there," Sheriff Buck said, frowning. "She might be a juvenile, Susan, but I can't say one way or the other. She hasn't stopped long enough for me to get a good look."

Carefully, Susan stepped back for a better view. If the girl was a juvenile she had no business in the county jail. Not that she wanted to get involved with this, Susan told herself, in the year since she and Buck had called off their engagement one could say they worked reasonably hard at a friendly, if not yet totally objective relationship.

"What are you holding her on?" she asked. Deputy Holt was now kneeling on the girl's thrashing, shapely bottom to keep it immobile while he fumbled for a handkerchief for his bitten hand.

It was Mose Holt who answered. "Miss Susan, there was two of them Scraggses. I brought them in for vagrancy and maybe assault the way the old lady was yelling, but the youngest Scraggs girl did a bolt and run just as I was getting them into the patrol car. The last time I saw her—the one they call Farrah Fawcett Scraggs—she was running fit to bust."

"*Scraggs?*" Susan turned to the sheriff. "Buck, you can't mean—"

He nodded curtly. "Devil Anse's granddaughters. And there's a lot of things I'd rather find under my Christmas tree than any of that tribe."

"I can't believe it," the caseworker murmured.

She turned back to the scantily clad hoyden who was now attempting to bite the deputy's wrist. The outlaw Scraggs clan, the curse of the Jackson County law-enforcement and social-welfare services, seldom ventured very far from their hideouts in the "hollers" of the Blue Ridge. The family patriarch—if you could call him that—old "Devil Anse" Scraggs, had been north Georgia's biggest bootlegger until he took up armed robbery, car theft, and other more sophisticated operations. At any rate his operational base was so deep in the mountains that even Buck's father, the first Sheriff Grissom, hadn't been able to rout him out.

Four months ago Sheriff Buck had managed to personally apprehend and send the oldest boy, Elvis Presley Scraggs, to state prison for car theft and attempted homicide, all accomplished one night when two of the older Scraggs boys had come to town for a little hell-raising.

Now Buck looked down at their struggling prisoner with an expression of bleak disapproval. "You'd think the old reprobate would spend money on clothes for his girl children. Especially one as—uh, well developed as this one. Go get a blanket, Mose," he told his deputy. "She's so cold she's blue around the edges."

"Well developed" was one way to describe it, Susan observed. She didn't like to give an official opinion, but it was obvious the girl was no juvenile. Not with those legs—and that body. Although, she had to admit, it was hard to tell: the Scraggs children attended school so irregularly one could never be certain of their ages.

"I wonder," she said, "if this is the one that somehow got as far as high school. Almost graduated, I think, before the grandfather found out and wouldn't let her finish. She was an interesting child, poor thing. Now, what was her name?"

"Better let her up," Buck ordered the deputy. "Now that Miss Susan is here we've got to be careful about inflicting physical pain, or—uh, mental anguish."

Susan shot him a sharp look. Since they'd broken off their engagement Buck couldn't resist a barb or two.

Moses Holt pried the girl off his chest. She sprang up from the floor in a fighting crouch. The deputy stepped back in time to miss a kick aimed at his crotch, when Buck suddenly made his move. Before the Scraggs girl knew what was happening he had seized her, levered her against the wall, then shoved her into the nearest cell. They heard it close and lock automatically.

"Dirty po-lice pigs!" The Scraggs granddaughter grabbed the bars of the cell with both hands, her pointed young breasts heaving. "Lowlife mudsuckers! You can't hold me in here, I ain't done nothing! When I get out of this place I'm going to make you sorry you ever did this to me!"

Deputy Holt brushed off the front of his uniform with shaking hands. "I was clean before I got near that lowdown female," he complained. "Ifn I was you, Sheriff, I'd get the matron to give that hellcat a bath with lye soap and a stiff brush!"

Susan Huddleston stepped forward. Clearly the girl didn't belong in jail, but neither could one discount the dangerous Scraggs factor, either. "Buck, I'd be very careful with all aspects of this," she warned.

Sheriff Buck only grunted. When he was still a young county deputy, before he'd taken over his father's job, he'd been called to the Nancyville middle school one day on a complaint of disorderly conduct and fighting. He'd gotten a faceful of scratches before the alleged culprit had taken off across the field in back of the school, never to be seen again. But before she'd hightailed it Buck had had a glimpse of a long-legged, scrawny vixen with the blackest eyes he'd ever seen.

Now, studying this female in the lockup, he couldn't swear she wasn't the same one. Although he tried not to look below her grimy neck where the old sweater and skimpy cotton dress left little to the imagination.

Susan said, "I don't suppose there's any doubt she's a Scraggs?"

The deputy promptly responded, "No doubt at all, Miss Susan. They call this one Scarlett O'Hara Scraggs. Her mamma gave them all fancy names. The sheriff here put one of her no-good relatives, Elvis Presley—"

"Yes, I know," Susan said quickly. It wasn't wise at that particular moment to bring up the sentence the oldest boy was doing in the state pen. And who had put him there. "I don't think you can charge her with a felony, Buck. Loitering's only a misdemeanor."

At her words the figure behind the bars stiffened.

"You can't keep me here!" the girl shrilled. Her black eyes flashed. "Yore fat old deputy whopped Demon for no reason at all and laid its head open, and my little sister ran off!"

"You did something to the little sister?" Buck turned to his deputy, frowning. "Who's this you whopped?"

Deputy Holt sucked on his bitten finger. "Buck, will you let me say something? These two Scraggs —*females*—was down by the post office this morning, sitting on the curb, making a nuisance, and their big monster dog done jumped Mrs. Stevens's cat and half tore it to death."

"Did not," the prisoner yelled. "That's a lie!"

"Mrs. Stevens called for police assistance," Mose went on doggedly. "When I got there these two were attempting forced entry on Mrs. Stevens's front door—"

"That old cow hit Farrah Fawcett," the prisoner shouted, "when we wasn't doing anything!"

"—threatening to assault Mrs. Stevens, and

8

throwing rocks at her house. This one told Mrs. Stevens she was going to—ah—"—Deputy Holt's face grew even redder—"snatch off certain parts of Mrs. Stevens's—ah, body."

"Tits!" the prisoner behind the bars screeched. "I told her I'd pull off her old flappy tits if she ever hit Farrah Fawcett again!"

Deputy Holt reached into his pocket and pulled out a handkerchief to wipe his face. "Buck, I never heard no young woman talk like that. I swear, there's just no telling the words that are going to come out of that mouth!"

"Where's my sister?" Scarlett O'Hara gripped the bars with both hands. "My little sister Farrie's run off in the cold, and she's lost and it's your fault, you old—"

Buck stepped toward her. "That's enough of that." The steely authority that had made his late father famous and which he had passed on to Buck in a considerable degree made the girl suddenly close her mouth. "Now let's hold it down," he ordered.

Scowling, the Scraggs girl tilted her head back to get a good look. The fluorescent light of the cell block illuminated Buck's square-jawed face and stern, unfriendly expression.

Buck was thinking Miss Scarlett O'Hara Scraggs looked wild and unmanageable. On the other hand, from her nearly bare feet to the top of her gypsy-black curls she projected so much—Buck's mind stumbled over the thought—well, *sexual attraction* that the effect on the public at large was worrisome.

"How old is the little sister?" he asked.

"Ten, eleven, somewheres around there," the deputy answered.

"And this one?"

Mose Holt shrugged. "She won't say."

Buck studied her. If the other Scraggs girl wasn't more than eleven years of age, then half the case was out of his jurisdiction. The younger half.

"Susan," he said, "I'd be obliged if you'd rout old Ancil Scraggs out of the hills and get him to come down and claim his relatives."

The words were no sooner out of his mouth than they were subjected to a truly anguished screech.

"Don't do that! Oh, please don't get my grandpa!" the figure behind the bars yelled. "Please, mister, I'll get that old witch another mangy cat in place of the one Demon tore up—me'n my little sister'll do anything! But don't let Devil Anse come for us!"

Scarlett O'Hara Scraggs clutched at the bars of the cell with an expression that was genuinely heartrending.

"Please, mister," she pleaded, "I'm nineteen years old, I'm full grown, I can do what I want, can't I? My little sister and I didn't do any harm sittin' on the curb waiting for the Greyhound bus that goes to Atlanta until that ole cat jumped on Demon. You gotta let me go, so I can go find Farrie!"

Buck turned to Susan. Who was staring at the prisoner, appalled.

"You gotta," the voice in the cell yelled belligerently. "We didn't break the law, me'n Farrah Fawcett! We were just *running away!*"

Two

SCARLETT WATCHED THE MAN SHE KNEW
by now was the sheriff talking to the tall blond
woman. Once he took her hand, but she quickly
moved it out of the way.

"I've never heard of a *runaway* Scraggs," the
woman was saying. "Although I suppose any child in
their right mind would want to get away from that
horrible crowd."

The big redheaded sheriff said, "This one's hardly
a child."

They both turned to study Scarlett. Who
hunched her shoulders in the gray jail blanket the
deputy had given her, and glared back.

Although Scarlett would never let them see it, she
was worried sick. Her little sister was somewhere
out there in the town of Nancyville, and it was
growing dark. Farrie didn't even have any money.
Scarlett had the sixty-three dollars for the bus tickets and the extra she'd taken when she'd raided the
black iron pot where Devil Anse kept his cash.

11

The only good thing Scarlett could think of was that at least Farrie had the good pair of shoes, the pink and white sneakers Scarlett had bought for her last summer. She'd kept the rubber sandals for herself. They were the reason her feet were so numb with cold now that she could hardly feel them.

The worst part, Scarlett knew, was that there was no telling where Farrie and Demon were now. And it was snowing, Scarlett had seen it as she was coming into the jail.

She heard the blonde say, "Well, Buck, you can't hold her on vagrancy, I don't care what that old crank, Della Stevens, told Mose."

"Assault, Susan," he told her, "not vagrancy. *Attempted assault.*"

She snorted. "*Assault* on Della's *cat?* It's as mean as old Della is!"

Scarlett pressed her face against the bars, listening. This wasn't turning out at all the way she'd planned it. By now the Greyhound bus to Atlanta had come and gone, instead of taking them away from Catfish Holler and their grandpa and the rest of the Scraggses. Farrie and her dog, Demon, were wandering around somewhere in Nancyville, and there she was. In the county jail!

The thought made Scarlett's mouth tremble, and she bit back hot tears. No need to cry, she told herself fiercely, you know it never gets you anywheres.

Nobody was coming to help. Help, she well knew, was for other people. Scraggses who cried got hit, whopped on the head, and made fun of.

12

Crying was the most useless thing anybody could do. Along with praying.

"The youngest girl should go into a shelter," the woman was saying. "That takes a court order." She hesitated. "Good heavens, relatives should be present in court. Can you imagine all those Scraggses—"

The sheriff's expression was grim. "That will be the day, when I have to round up the Scraggses to appear on a runaway case. Believe me, Susan, if I ever get them into court I'm going to prosecute the whole tribe for manslaughter, hijacking, armed robbery—everything else they're wanted for."

Scarlett studied the sheriff with narrowed, suspicious eyes. He didn't talk about Devil Anse the way other people did. Like they'd do anything to stay out of his way.

"I just can't turn her loose, Susan. Listen, can't you put her over in the Hardee County shelter with her little sister? That is, when we find her."

"Are you kidding?" The woman turned to him. "Buck, you're not going to make me give up my Christmas vacation! Why, even if I could find somebody brave enough to take in a couple of Scraggses over the holidays—which is highly unlikely— there's the prospect that Devil Anse would be coming to town to claim them. Ugh! Why do I keep thinking in terms of armed attack, siege, home invasion, ambush—"

"Don't be melodramatic, Susan," the sheriff said coldly. "It's not called for."

"Melodramatic?" The social worker put her hands

on her hips and faced him. "Look, I didn't volunteer for this. You called *me*, remember?"

Scarlett was thinking the woman was right. At any minute now Devil Anse would find out that his granddaughters were missing. And so was his money.

She took a deep breath. She was never going back, neither was Farrie. That's what she'd promised.

"I'm not going to miss my meeting in Atlanta," the woman was saying firmly. "And this girl isn't in my jurisdiction, anyway. Frankly, I was glad to get Scarlett O'Hara off my hands when she left high school. Buck, just do what your dad always did."

"Don't drag my father into this," the sheriff growled, "I know how you feel about him, Susan."

"I wasn't dragging your father into anything! Besides, I know your mother wouldn't object."

The sheriff's jaw tightened. "You don't have to criticize my mother, either."

She stared at him. "Look, Buck, I know the Scraggses are not the most rewarding project to get involved in here at Christmas. I've chased them from one end of the county to the other and they're hopeless. The men won't let the women and children have any contact with strangers, they're too afraid the government will find their stolen-car chop shops and the rest of the rackets they're into up there in the hills, and prosecute them." A little pleadingly, she touched him on the sleeve. "I've paid good money to attend my meeting and have my holiday, Buck, don't ask me to give it up. Anyway, the county doesn't have the money to put the

Scraggs girls up in a motel, much less pay a matron to supervise them. And you can't leave them alone. I don't see that you have any other choice."

The sheriff looked like a thundercloud. The last thing he wanted for Christmas was Devil Anse's granddaughters. "Dammit, Susan, if it comes to that, I'd pay their motel bill myself!"

She suddenly looked at her wristwatch. "Good heavens," she exclaimed, "I haven't got time for this! It's a good thing I'm all packed and my bags are in my car outside."

She started toward Scarlett, the sheriff following. "Susan," he was saying, "why don't we leave her here in the cell block and see how things work out?"

"You can't do that. Scarlett's not a criminal. And as a Scraggs, she's got enough against her as it is. Scarlett," she said, "do you understand what we've been talking about? When your sister is found the sheriff can't keep her in jail. And we don't want to send you back to your grandfather without a court hearing. Sheriff Grissom agrees with me that we need to move you out of here."

"Now just a minute," the sheriff said, "I didn't say—"

"Scarlett O'Hara," the woman went on, "Sheriff Grissom has very kindly offered to take you home with him."

Three

A GUST OF WIND SWEPT INTO NANCYVILLE from the heights of Makim's Mountain, making the tinsel garland on Main Street whirl in the winter light. The same blast swept across the windshield of the Blazer with enough sleet to blot out Sheriff Buck's vision. Muttering under his breath, he switched on the wipers, then turned the heater to Defrost.

Beside him the Scraggs girl was still clawing at the Blazer's locked door. It had taken a good bit of Buck's strength and all of Susan Huddleston's guile to get her into the county police vehicle, and once inside Scarlett had been sure she'd been tricked, that she was under arrest and on her way to the state pen. Screaming, she'd attacked the inside of the Blazer in a fury. She was still at it.

"You gotta let me out of here, I ain't done anything!" She pounded the door handles and window glass with both fists. "I mean it, you gotta let me out! I gotta go look for my little sister!"

"Stop that!" The screaming in the close confines of the Blazer was fraying Buck's temper; he was used to more orderly prisoners. Except, he reminded himself, Scarlett Scraggs wasn't exactly a prisoner. "Sit down," he ordered. "And act decent!"

As he said it, Buck realized that "decent" wasn't a word that one could use to command the Scraggses. Unless he was mistaken, Scarlett's mother was the Scraggs who'd left Devil Anse's youngest son to run away with a country and western guitar player from Nashville. It was unlikely that Elvis Presley, Farrah Fawcett, or Scarlett herself had been exposed to any sort of stable home life.

For the second time that afternoon Buck experienced an unsettling nervous cramp in his stomach. His mother—whatever her past experiences with his father's Christmas strays and vagrants from the county jail—had never coped with a true Scraggs. Bringing this half-wild creature home, not to mention the other sister when she showed up, filled Buck with foreboding. And he was not used to feeling that way. Not since Susan Huddleston announced she was calling off their engagement.

That, he told himself sourly, was another thing. He still couldn't fathom how his ex-fiancée could make him feel so guilty, when the damned engagement was over and done with a long time ago. He should have put the Scraggses up in a motel. They could have found some way around regulations.

The girl beside him had stopped banging on the door. Now she slumped in her seat, substituting the earsplitting howls for subdued, but just as nerve-racking moaning. Buck glanced at her. Her head was bent, her face hidden by a mop of hair that fell forward.

"Farrie's out there, in all that snow and cold." A gulping sound that might have been a sob broke from her. "And you're gonna take me someplace"—she turned, the gypsy eyes gleaming at him balefully—"to do whatever it is you think you're gonna do to me!"

"What I'm going to *do* to you?" Buck stepped on the brakes in surprise. The Blazer bucked in protest, then skidded sideways on the sleety road. Scarlett Scraggs clutched the dashboard and screamed.

Buck snarled something under his breath.

"There, you *cussed*," she screeched. "I heard what you just said!"

At that moment the county dispatcher called on the police radio. "Sheriff, your mother's been trying to get you."

"Even I know a sheriff," the Scraggs female was screaming, "ain't supposed to cuss like that!"

"Dammit," he barked, "will you *shut up?*"

"Sheriff, I'm only trying to do my job," the voice of the dispatcher said.

"Not you, George." Buck had tried to get his mother on the telephone before he left the jail, but the line at home had been persistently busy. "Listen," he said into the radio, "if my mother calls back—"

"You got no right to talk to me like that!" Scarlett Scraggs maintained at the top of her lungs. "I want to know where you're taking me!"

"Sheriff?" The dispatcher's tone was cautious. "You got a—ah, prisoner with you?"

Buck was aware how all this sounded, so, he was sure, did Scarlett Scraggs. "No prisoner, George. I'm taking care of some of Susan Huddleston's confounded problems. If my mother calls again, tell her to use the cellular phone."

Buck was well aware that it had been a long time since his mother had put up any strays from the jail. That was something his dad had made a tradition when he was alive. Sheriff Buck Grissom, Sr., had been a law unto himself in the Georgia hills.

One year, Buck remembered, his dad had brought home a whole poverty-stricken family of migrant workers stranded on the highway when their old truck broke down. They'd had all seven of them for a week, straight through the New Year's holiday. His mother had nearly gone crazy.

His passenger was wrestling with the door handle again. "You're taking me someplace where my little sister'll never find me!" she wailed. "I'll never see Farrie again!"

"This is a county police vehicle," he warned her, "the doors lock automatically. You won't get that open no matter how hard you pound on it."

The Blazer turned into Main Street. Traffic was light in the bad weather, and Nancyville was not a big enough town for a real rush hour. In spite of the aluminum holiday messages strung across the thoroughfare, the central area was bleak. Just beyond the R&R Variety Store, the Valley Bank, and Nancyville Hardware was the red brick pile that had formerly been the town's textile mill, closed since the 1970's.

The old mill was a reminder of all the jobs lost,

all the people born and bred in the mountains who'd gone from Nancyville south to Atlanta and Birmingham or north to Chicago. The blighting presence of the mill was the reason the Nancyville Downtown Merchants' Association needed the living manger scene at the courthouse to bring folks in to shop, so they wouldn't go over to the giant mall on the interstate.

"Listen," Buck said, relenting a little, "I've got practically my entire force out on the road looking for your little sister. When they find her I'm going to turn both of you over to my mother, and she'll look after you until Sus—until Miss Huddleston gets back."

Even as he spoke Buck realized Susan's holiday would not be over until well after New Year's. The prospect of being stuck through a full week of Christmas with any part of the Scraggs clan was something that rendered him almost numb.

Scraggses all through Christmas.

Unseeing, Buck turned off the windshield wipers. The sleet had stopped but the sky looked as though a storm was brewing up north in the Smokies. Bad weather was all the county police needed these last days before Christmas.

This infernal mess was all Susan Huddleston's fault, Buck thought, leaving town and abandoning her job to take a Christmas holiday! Now that they no longer had any plans for marriage, Susan obviously felt she could do as she pleased. What remained between them wasn't the friendly, cooperative relationship Buck thought they'd agreed

21

upon. On the contrary, Susan could be downright hostile and treacherous. Like she was this afternoon.

Buck supposed that like most couples they had broken up with their share of hard words. Certainly they'd always fought over the day-and-night demands of her social-work job, and Susan still didn't know how to cook a decent meal. She didn't seem to have enough interest in it to want to learn how. Buck had made it plain he was damned if he was going to settle for a life of microwave dinners.

Susan's reply, which in his opinion wasn't really any sort of reply, was that if he felt that way he could learn to cook himself. "Rigid," was the word she'd flung at him. And "pompous." And "father-dominated."

That last really irritated him. How could "father-dominated" apply to somebody whose father was already dead?

Buck reached out for the cellular phone on the dashboard. When he tried home he got the same busy signal. Scarlett Scraggs sat hunched in the corner, watching him as he turned the Blazer into Magnolia Street and the extension that climbed Makim's Mountain. She sniffled from time to time, wiping her eyes sullenly with the back of her hand. Finally the Blazer bumped into the driveway and the house came into sight. The girl beside him promptly lunged forward in the seat, eyes wide. "Is that your house? All *that*?"

Buck made an affirmative noise. The Grissom house sat on the side of the mountain overlooking Nancyville Valley. It had been a trapper's log cabin when the first Blankenships migrated to Georgia from Virginia in the early eighteen hundreds and decided to build on the slope for the view.

In the next generation, when most of the valley's Cherokee landowners had been driven out and their land confiscated, the Blankenships had prospered. By the end of a decade Blankenships owned the whole valley and founded the town of Nancyville, naming it after the second Thomas Blankenship's bride.

By the time of the Civil War, wealthy Blankenships added an upper story and four white Greek Revival columns to their mansion. These were torn down a few years later to make way for a renovation in the grand Victorian Gothic style, with a turret tower, two ornamental balconies, jigsaw work all around, and a huge front porch. In the 1950's the last remaining Blankenship sold the cotton mill to northern investors and moved to Los Angeles. When Buck's father bought the place the farmland it once stood on was gone, the downstairs rooms were being used for hay storage, and the roof had fallen in. It had taken years to restore it.

Buck's mother, slim as a girl in a red suit and matching coat, was standing in the middle of the driveway, several suitcases around her. Buck felt another ominous pang in the bottom of his stomach.

He cut the Blazer's engine and got out. "Mother, what the devil?"

"Oh, thank goodness, there you are. I've been trying to get you on the telephone for over an hour, but nobody seemed to be able to find you. Never mind." Alicia Blankenship Grissom tugged at her shoulder-strap handbag to pull it around to her

23

front. "I think I'm all together. Have I got my credit cards? Yes, I have, here they are. The airline said I could pick up my tickets in Gainesville. Good heavens, I had no idea how expensive it was, buying a ticket at the last minute!"

She lifted her head to look past Buck to the Blazer. "Who's that, darling? Have you got a prisoner?"

"Yes. No. Mother," Buck said hurriedly, "you're not going anywhere. You can't."

"When I couldn't get you on the telephone," his mother said, snapping shut her purse, "I called Camilla Farnsworth, and she's going to drive me down to Gainesville. So it's all right, dear. You won't have to leave work to take me."

Buck had been listening impatiently. "Mother, look at me, will you? Remember how Dad used to bring people home from the jail at Christmastime?"

"Willie, darling," his mother interrupted, "don't start on anything right now, I have a plane to catch."

He couldn't believe his mother thought she was taking a plane. "Mother, I've brought this—" Buck turned to look at the Blazer and Scarlett O'Hara Scraggs making contorted faces behind the windshield. "I've brought you a gi—a young woman— home for Christmas." Buck couldn't bring himself to say "one of Devil Anse's granddaughters." "Actually, Susan Huddleston, the social worker—"

"Yes, darling," his mother said, lifting one of her suitcases, "I remember. You used to be engaged to her."

"Well, she's going out of town on a holiday, of all

24

the imbecilic ideas, and I have this Christmas vagrant I have to place. Susan—uh, regulations say I can't keep her in jail." He ran his fingers through his hair. His mother didn't appear to be listening. "Actually, there are two of them. Sisters."

His mother had walked a few steps with her nylon suit bag and pressed it into his hand. "Sweetheart, I really haven't got time to listen." The wind ruffled her shoulder-length hair, making her look even younger and prettier. "Willie, your sister's poor husband is in the hospital with a broken leg and possible skull fracture, and Sheila's half out of her mind. Christmas is coming, the children are out of school, and goodness only knows how they're going to manage with Sheila in the hospital looking after James. Camilla is coming—oh, there's her car now." His mother started down the driveway. "Get the other bag, too, will you, dear?"

Buck trailed after his mother carrying her luggage. His mind wasn't working. Apparently his sister had just had a terrible accident.

"Mother, how did it happen?" Camilla Farnsworth's Buick pulled up behind the Blazer. "Is Sheila all right?"

"*James* has the skull fracture, dear," his mother said gently. "At least it might be a skull fracture, they don't know yet. Sheila's the one who needs me. Just put my bags in the trunk, will you?"

Camilla Farnsworth handed her trunk key to Buck. "Hi, Sheriff." Her smile faded as her eyes found the Blazer. "Good grief! Is that one of your prisoners?"

Buck stared at his mother's friend. "Camilla, you can't take my mother anywhere right now," he said, desperate. "The county caseworker's gone out of town and I have this possible vagrancy-and-assault I have to place, and her sister, too, if she shows up. I need Mother to take care of them."

Camilla took the travel bag out of his hand and put it in the trunk. "Just like your dad used to do, Junior? It figures."

He didn't like the way that sounded. "Mother never minded doing it," he said stiffly. "Besides, I can't keep them in the jail, the younger sister is a juvenile." He remembered Scarlett's insinuations at the top of her lungs. "And it wouldn't look right for me to be out here in the house all alone with them."

His mother came up behind them. "Oh Willie, you'll manage, you always do. Don't worry so much. If they're sisters they can chaperone each other. Camilla's invited you for Christmas dinner and you can take your prisoners with you."

Camilla grimaced. "Just promise me they haven't done anything terrible. All the Farnsworths are coming, and serial killers would really shake them up."

"Very funny, Camilla." Buck followed them to the front of the car. "They're not prisoners. You haven't given me a chance to explain."

His mother turned to kiss him good-bye. "Darling, don't fuss. The freezer is full of microwave dinners and there's plenty of beer in the refrigerator. I didn't quite get the tree trimmed, I'm afraid there are boxes all over the living room, but I put your

26

presents out where you can find them. Don't forget to call me Christmas morning. Sheila's number is—"

"Mother, I'm not three years old, I know her number." The first unpleasant shock was waning. Buck was beginning to feel bad about the way he had reacted to what was, after all, a family emergency. His mother was doing the right thing, dropping everything to fly off to Chicago to be with his sister.

On the other hand, he didn't know what the hell he was going to do for the next nine or ten days. His stomach clenched just thinking about it.

"Let me know how Sheila is," he said, as he closed the Buick's door.

"James," his mother corrected mechanically. She suddenly looked past him and her eyes widened. Scarlett O'Hara had climbed over the driver's seat and out of the Blazer. A gust of wind took her skimpy skirt, whipping it about incredible bare legs. She clutched the old purple sweater tight about her upper body. "Oh my," Buck's mother said.

Buck turned. "Yes, that's what I wanted to tell—"

It was too late. Camilla had already put the Buick in gear. His mother blew a kiss from the open window as the car moved forward.

The big car rolled down the driveway and turned into the mountain road. Buck heard footsteps behind him.

"Was that your mother?" Scarlett Scraggs wanted to know. "You don't look much like her."

Buck turned. She stood with her arms wrapped around her body, curls whipping in the wind like a dark flag. Her eyes were rimmed with thick, sooty lashes, a pouty lip lifted over white teeth. Perfect

27

teeth, he saw. When she'd probably never seen a dentist in her whole life.

"I look like my dad," he heard himself say.

He had just realized he wasn't going to wait for the other Scraggs sister to show up, he was going to have to do something. He could call neighboring county government services, if their offices were still open, and see if he could find a place for the Scraggs females to stay the night. Even down in Gainesville, if that was all he could get.

"Come on, I've got to get to the telephone," he started to say, when something came through the snow-filled air and hit him hard on one shoulder.

Buck staggered. There was a snuffling, horrible noise that seemed to conjure up the soundtrack of all the teen slasher movies he'd ever seen. A snarling, slavering force bore him to earth.

He fell flat on his face in the driveway and hit his nose and mouth. He could feel the first trickle of blood. Buck had only breath enough for a strangled half-shout. Whatever it was, it was strong enough to hold him down so that he could hardly move. Hot breath roared in his ear.

"Don't do it!" someone was screaming. "Demon, get off!"

With an effort, Buck pried himself to his elbows while human hands yanked at his hair, pulling his head back.

"Don't move," another voice was yelling. "She won't hurt you ifn you just lie still!"

A face came into view. It was the strangest face Buck had ever seen, all huge eyes and wild hair, the head perched on a neck like a skeletal stalk. He managed to reach under him and drag his gun from the holster.

As he did so, the apparition leaned down and put her face next to his and yelled, "Scarlett, do something! He's gonna shoot my dog!"

Four

SOME UNSEEN HAND PRIED THE NIGHT-
mare thing from Buck's back. He rolled over and
sprang to his feet, gun held out in both hands and
aimed at, he found, a strange, stick-thin, goblin
child about ten years old wearing a ragged football
jacket. She promptly flung herself on Scarlett
Scraggs.

"Oh, lordee," the ragged child sobbed, "we just
nearly didn't find you, Scarlett! Me'n Demon was
watching the police station, and when we saw you
get in that Blazer I knew we was goners!" She
wrapped her arms around Scarlett's waist and laid
her frizzy head against her breast. "How was anybody gonna find their way following a car up this
ole mountain, even with a good tracker like Demon?"

Carefully, Buck turned to cover the other target, a
giant black dog that now sat with its tongue lolling
out, regarding him interestedly. Buck immediately
recognized the animal as the force that had sprung

31

on him and borne him to the ground a few moments earlier.

The second thing he saw was that blood from his nose was now pouring steadily down the front of his uniform to mix with mud, snow, and a trace of engine oil from the drive. He removed one hand from his police special .38 long enough to tentatively wipe his nose. A fresh flood of red showed he'd only made it worse.

Scarlett Scraggs was talking to the ragged child. "Well, you made it, honey, you don't have to cry," she was saying in a surprisingly gentle voice. "But you shouldn't have run off that way when we had that fight with that old witch. You gotta stick close, Farrie, or I'm going to lose you and Demon. Then we'll *never* get to Atlanta."

Farrie.

This, then, was the missing little sister. Buck put his gun back in his holster and straightened up.

"I'm just so glad Demon is such a good tracker," the child sobbed. "She can find *anybody*. But we had to stop and look and look and look down all the streets and roads, and I was so scared—I thought we'd never find you!" She twisted her head to look at Buck. "He isn't going to shoot Demon, is he?" She clutched Scarlett anxiously. "Demon just jumped on him because he's po-lice. Like the other one. Demon wasn't going to hurt him!"

Buck grimly regarded the dog, now lying quietly with its nose between its massive paws. "If that thig attacks me again, ids going to be the last time." He had trouble talking because his nose was bleeding freely and he had to cover it with one hand. "Cob on, bode of you. I need to teledphone."

Scarlett smoothed the child's snow-flecked hair back from her face. "Farrie, you've been out in the cold for hours," she clucked. "I bet you're gonna get sick."

Her sister clung to her, staring at Buck. "Why are we going inside his house?" she wanted to know. "What's he going to do with us?"

"Yeds, house," Buck ordered, pointing to it. "Got to call off APB now thad your sidster showed up."

"Nothing," Scarlett said to the child, "he's not going to do anything. We're supposed to be staying here with his mother." She bent to take the dog by the collar. "Only his mother left."

Buck stepped in between. "That thig's not going in he house. It stayds outside."

At his tone the huge dog rose to its feet, the hair on its back standing up in an unfriendly manner. Buck's scowl had sent Farrah Fawcett Scraggs scuttling to hide behind Scarlett. "What's wrog with her?" he demanded. "Ids she hurt?"

The look from Scarlett's black eyes was withering. "There's nothing wrong with my little sister!" She took the child's hand and started for the house.

"Somethig's wrog," Buck insisted, following. "She limps. She been hurt?"

"She doesn't limp!" Scarlett was pulling her sister along rather roughly. "There's nothing wrong with Farrie. She only limps when she forgets!"

"Whed she forgets?" Buck opened the front door. A rush of wonderfully warm air reached out to them. "She only limps whed she *forgets*?"

Scarlett pushed past him into the hallway. "Oh, it's so *warm*," she gasped. "We nearabout froze out there!"

The child squeezed past him, the dog in tow.

"Dammid!" Buck snatched at the animal with his free hand but missed.

At that moment Buck knew he was going to have to do something about his injured nose and never mind the Scraggs sisters; they were in the house and safe enough for the time being. But he was a bloody mess.

He started for the kitchen to search for paper towels to stanch his nosebleed. While there, he stopped long enough to ring up a few numbers in the hope of finding the Scraggs sisters a place for the night. The neighboring county's juvenile office was closed for the day, but he was able to get the Hardee County sheriff on his mobile telephone.

"Buck, you're not pulling my leg, are you?" the Hardee sheriff boomed. "Scraggs? Like some of Devil Anse's crowd? Hey, this is Christmas coming up, not Halloween! You want to get my jail dynamited? Our social worker run out of town? Call me back when you've sobered up, boy!"

Buck was too tired to think of a reply. And the Hardee sheriff had a point. He thanked him and hung up. The prospects of placing the Scraggses somewhere, at least for the night, were growing dim.

Buck came out of the kitchen with a roll of paper towels under his arm. The front hallway was empty, the house suspiciously quiet. Where the devil had they gone to? he wondered.

The door to the dining room was open. He thought he could hear voices: Scarlett O'Hara's husky contralto, the gnomish child's squeaky rasp.

"Oh, Scarlett, it's a tree!" As he grew closer he knew this was the little sister. "Isn't this the most beautiful house you ever saw? And a *real* Christmas tree, to go with this *real* house!"

There were curious rustling noises. "His mother went off and left all these things around," he heard the other one say. "See, all over the floor."

Buck moved into the doorway.

Like many houses built in the nineteenth century the dining room and parlor were connected by paneled doors, now open to make one big room—a beautiful room with high ceilings, Victorian plasterwork, and parquet floors covered with reproductions of nineteenth-century Brussels carpet.

The house represented Buck's mother's years of hard work and decorating skill. Just as it did the love in his father's original gift of it to her. The furniture was Victorian reproductions, as were the gilded Venetian mirrors, the green velvet draperies now looped with fancy red and gold Christmas garlands.

Buck could see Scarlett O'Hara Scraggs was right. Alicia Grissom had dropped everything in her hurry to leave for Chicago. The rooms were strewn with Christmas ornament boxes, partly wrapped gift packages, and ropes of tree tinsel. In the parlor area the blue spruce Christmas tree that Buck had put up towered over everything, half-finished.

The two girls had their backs to him, bent over the boxes. Buck was suddenly aware that Scarlett wore a sweater with holes in it over a faded dress and was bare-legged, her feet in rubber Japanese sandals, purple with cold. The child had on a frayed magenta football jacket over either a long shirt or a very short dress, it was difficult to tell, and baggy lime-colored tights with snow-stained sneakers.

Buck winced. This was not just the signs of poverty; the southern Appalachians were full of people who had been poor for generations. This was something worse.

The child straightened up, a tree ornament in her hand. "When we get to Atlanta," she said in a dreamy voice, "we're going to have to work hard and make enough money to find a house like this to live in." She lurched her way to the tree and fastened the ornament on it.

"Well, first I gotta get a job." Scarlett's voice was less hopeful. "I don't know how to do much, and I missed my high school diploma."

"Oh, you're going to get a good job, Scarlett," the child told her, "because you're so smart. Even ole Devil Anse Grandpa says that. And you'll make enough money and we'll be able to buy a car, and go travelin'."

Scarlett watched her sister as she dug another ornament out of the box and fixed it to the tree.

"First we got to get there," she said softly. "We didn't do so good today when we missed the bus because your dog was trying to kill that old woman's cat. It hasn't done you a bit of good, either, being out in the cold. Come here, Farrie." She pulled the child to her and laid her hand on her forehead. "You're turning red. I just know you're gonna get sick."

Buck stepped into the room. "What do you mean, she's going to be sick?" The little Scraggs was shivering all over, even Buck could see that. "Does she get sick often?"

Scarlett Scraggs turned to him, her arm protectively around the child. "She's been out in the cold, that's all." She hesitated, then set her jaw. "I've got to put her to bed somewhere. You don't have to do us a favor. We can put up most anywhere."

"I don't know what you mean by 'anywhere.'" Buck frowned down at Farrah Fawcett Scraggs. He thought of pneumonia. He wouldn't put it past her; the kid was like a skeleton, anyway. "My sister's old room," he said hurriedly. "Let's go."

Buck dropped the paper towels. Before she could run from him he seized the littler Scraggs and lifted her in his arms. He was startled at how weightless she was, even with the soggy football jacket, which gave out a sour odor.

"Upstairs," Buck said tersely. "Turn right."

He argued with himself about calling a doctor. Not Dr. Henson who served the county jail, that was too complicated because other agencies were involved, like Susan Huddleston's. Yet if he called his own family physician Buck had a good idea of the explaining he would have to do.

Under his breath he groaned.

As he mounted the stairs with Farrah Fawcett Scraggs in his arms, Scarlett trailing behind, Buck was struck with another thought. It was six o'clock. Dinnertime. No matter how soon or late the doctor got there, or even if he decided to wait to see what happened before calling one, there was one thing certain.

"Oh hell," Buck muttered, "we've got to eat. Now it looks like I'm going to have to *cook*."

Five

"SCARLETT, TELL ME ABOUT WHEN I WAS A baby." Farrie moved the paper plates with the remains of the pizza and baked beans they'd had for dinner to the other side of the bed. "Oh, ain't this the most beautiful room?" she breathed. "Did you hear the sheriff say it used to belong to his sister before she got married?" She suddenly jerked up in the bed, excited. "Just think about living here all the time in this old house, and sleeping in this bed with posts all around it and curtains hung over the top!"

"It's called a tester." Scarlett got up, collected their plates, and carried them to a safe place on the Victorian bowfront bureau. "You can buy them at K Mart."

Farrie shook her head. "This didn't come from K Mart. And the bathroom's got a window where you can sit in the bathtub and look out and see trees like there wasn't nobody else in the world to see you sitting there buck naked except for a whole tub full of good-smelling bubbles!"

"Anybody else," Scarlett said, frowning. "We said when we left Catfish Holler we was—*were*—going to try to talk right, like people on television, remember? And not like a Scraggs."

"Anybody, then." Farrie closed her eyes, blissful. "Oh Scarlett, wouldn't you like to be lucky enough to live in a house like this?"

Scarlett sat down on the side of the bed and studied her little sister. Farrie's freshly shampooed hair stood out around her hair in a wiry bush. She was not a pretty girl, Scarlett always told herself, but Farrie had her own sort of looks. It was true her cheekbones stuck out and her jaw was a little crooked, but she had big, lively eyes that lit up her face. And that grin, Scarlett thought. When Farrie was happy, no one could resist that pixie grin.

Still, in the last few years Scarlett had begun to wonder if her sister would have a chance when she grew up to find someone who would see something special in her. And want to love her, and marry her. Scarlett worried a lot about it. The Scraggses didn't have much luck that way. And Farrie had even less.

She could see Farrie's cheeks were flushed as though she had a fever. It was due, probably, to what they'd been through, a lot for someone like Farrie, who'd been raised in a broken-down trailer on the side of a mountain in the wildest part of the Blue Ridge. From her look she was so wound up she probably wouldn't go to sleep until after midnight.

"Yeah, it's a nice house," Scarlett agreed. She pulled the covers up to her sister's neck and patted them in place. "I thought you wanted me to tell you the story about when you were a baby."

The little girl nodded quickly, eyes shining. Scarlett had been telling this story ever since Farrie had been old enough to listen, but she never seemed to tire of it.

"Well," Scarlett began, "I never had a doll of my own when I was your age." She was thinking that she was so tired herself she could hardly hold her eyes open. In a minute she was going to crawl into that big, soft bed beside Farrie and get some sleep. "No, I forgot, I had a doll once." She'd pretended not to remember; the story always went this way. And Farrie nodded as she always did. "I was about your age when the Baptists over at Toccoa sent a Sunday-school bus around the mountain hollers at Christmastime for kids who didn't—"

She paused, waiting. Farrie said, "Didn't have any Christmas. Like us."

"That's right. She was a real nice doll." Scarlett's voice grew wistful. "She had eyes that would open and close and real eyelashes. You never saw a doll like that one, it was so pretty. They gave me a scarf and mittens somebody had made, and a bag of candy, too. Only that year Bubba Scraggs, he was your daddy's brother, he took my Baptist church doll almost as soon as I got home and broke it when he was stinking drunk. I hadn't had it long at all. So when Mamma brought you back from the hospital I thought you looked like my doll. You was just about the same size."

"I wasn't pretty," Farrie put in. "Not like your doll."

Scarlett looked thoughtful, which was part of the game. "Well, no, not at first. You was just a little

41

scrunched-up bundle in a blanket they left laying there on the bed because you were sickly. First thing you know Mamma said she couldn't stand it no more, she was tired of the Scraggses, and she upped and went off with a guitar player from Nashville."

"And I cried." Farrie was smiling. "I was a puny baby."

Scarlett patted her kneecap under the bedspread. "Yes, honey, you cried day and night, I just hated to hear it. But I didn't give up on you."

Never in all the years since then had Scarlett told Farrie the truth. That the reason their mother had run off was that she didn't want the baby the doctors had said might not live. The little bundle that lay on the bed and cried for hours had skin a dark slate color and it aimlessly jerked its matchstick arms and legs in a way that even Scarlett could see wasn't normal.

"After a while I just picked you up and washed you," Scarlett went on, "and carried you around like a real dollbaby. Nobody said anything, I guess they were just glad you stopped crying. I cleaned out the baby bottles and fed you canned milk and corn syrup like they told Mamma to do in the hospital. And I thought you were the best little doll anybody ever had. You were my very own."

No matter what happened Scarlett would never tell Farrie of that terrible night when Devil Anse and one of her uncles had come to take the baby, without even saying what they were going to do with it. "It won't live much longer," her grandpa had said. "You're just wasting your time with it, girl."

Farrie said, "You took care of me and you weren't much older than me."

"That's right, I was about nine." Scarlett had fought like a tiger when her grandpa and her uncle tried to take the baby away, and finally they'd let it be. "Going to die, anyway," was what Devil Anse had said.

Thinking of it made Scarlett uneasy. "Look, it's all well and good for the sheriff to put us up like this," she said, "but don't forget we gotta get out of here. Devil Anse is going to find us sooner or later."

If her grandpa did what he said he would, Farrie would be left to fend for herself in Catfish Hollow. And Scarlett knew how long that would last. They would let Farrie get sick and die, as her grandpa had meant for her to do when she was a baby.

"He's not going to catch us, Scarlett!" Farrie hauled herself up in bed, eyes blazing. "Listen, we don't have to go anywheres. We just got the best Christmas present anybody ever had in the whole world, only we just didn't see it!"

Scarlett made a warning cluck against her teeth. "Farrie, for goodness' sake, you're gonna be sick if you don't slide down in that bed and close your eyes. Go to sleep—I don't want to be up all night with you, I'm tired and need some rest myself."

But Farrie seized the sleeve of her sweater in both hands. "Scarlett, we could live right here in this house. Right here in Nancyville. We wouldn't *have* to go to a far-off place like Atlanta!"

Scarlett pried her hand away. She brushed the sticky pizza crumbs off her front and stood up.

"Don't talk like that, Farrie. We can't stay here, this house belongs to the sheriff."

Her sister got to her knees in the middle of the bed. "Don't you see it, Scarlett?" she shrilled. "The sheriff's house is the last place Devil Anse will come looking for us. And if he does—why you know that big tough sheriff won't let him do anything. No sirree! Scarlett, this here place is *safer* than Atlanta!"

Scarlett leaned over and pushed her sister back down against the pillows. "Farrie, I swear, I'm getting worried. I don't think you've got that much fever, but you're talking out of your head."

"No I'm not! We can have this house and the sheriff can live here, too. All you got to do is marry him!"

"*What?*"

Scarlett straightened up to stare at her.

"Yes!" Farrie jerked her head up and down violently. "Scarlett, he's good-looking," she pleaded, "it wouldn't be so hard to do. Not like the ones that are always pestering you around Grandpa's place. And he's the *sheriff*, you can't get no safer than that. Besides, I think he likes you—he's always looking at you when he thinks you don't know it."

"Good Lord." Scarlett sat down abruptly on the edge of the bed. "When did you start thinking like this?"

Farrie looked at her solemnly. "Didn't you say if we ever wanted to live like other people we had to run away from Catfish Holler? That if we stayed up there with Devil Anse and the rest we'd end up no better than they was—*were?* Well, I guess it was while I was taking a bath in that bathroom where you can look out into the woods, and thinking about that big room downstairs with the Christmas tree in it that it came to me. And the way I feel now in this big beautiful bed, all warm with the curtains hanging over me, just like a princess. All of a sudden I had this idea that you'n me could live here if you was married to the sheriff, and nobody could put us out in the cold. And Devil Anse would be too scared to come here, too!"

"Farrie." Scarlett put her hand to her sister's forehead. The skin was hot to the touch. "You gotta stop it."

"And I knew just then," her little sister went on, determined, "that if dreams could come true, I knew what my dream would be. That we could be a family, Scarlett, like other folks. With a beautiful big house."

"You're not making sense," Scarlett said. "I don't care how much you dream about it, I can't make a man like that—*sheriff*—marry me. That's the dumbest thing I ever heard of."

"It's not any worse than what Devil Anse was going to make you do," Farrie cried. "That was why you ran away, remember?"

Scarlett didn't answer. She stood up, went to the dresser, and gathered up the paper plates.

"That's what's so good about my idea, Scarlett." Farrie hiked her frail body up on the pillows. "This way you can marry the sheriff and get this big house, and we can stay together."

Scarlett snorted. "Until the sheriff's mamma comes home. She lives here, too, you know."

"She can just go live someplace else," Farrie insisted. "Or I'll share with her. I don't mind sharing a room with somebody's mamma. Oh, Scarlett, when we left Catfish Holler you said you was—were—going to take care of me. You said you was going to give us a whole new life!"

Scarlett stood biting her lip. She'd promised all that. But at the time she hadn't known what a slim chance they'd have getting it. A better life was a sometime thing. Especially for a Scraggs.

She'd been desperate, though, to get Farrie away from Devil Anse. That was the first step, and the hardest. Now Scarlett could see how a lot of things could go wrong. Missing the bus to Atlanta was one. Landing in jail was another. Inwardly she flinched. She never wanted *that* to happen again.

On the other hand Scarlett had to admit that she'd never imagined they'd end up at the sheriff's house. She was still trying to figure it out. Now, with Farrie wanting to live in it, things were growing even more complicated.

"Just lie back down, Farrie." Scarlett gathered the paper plates to take them downstairs. "And stop having these crazy ideas."

She started for the door, then heard a quiet sob.

Scarlett stopped short. The problem was, Farrie knew Scarlett would do just about anything for her.

"All right," Scarlett sighed, giving in. "If you promise to lie down in bed and get some sleep, I'll try to think of something."

"That's what you always say, Scarlett," Farrie reminded her.

That, too, was true.

* * *

The downstairs hallway was quiet, and a blue light shone from an open door. Scarlett heard voices and music from a television set.

Down here the house had the faint scent of flowers, furniture wax, and pine boughs. It was almost too warm. A faint whoosh startled Scarlett until she realized it was the furnace turning on.

The whole house was toasty hot, she thought, relishing it. People didn't know how lucky they were to be warm all the time. In the muted darkness the crystal hall light shone over her head, and the candlesticks on the hall table glittered.

It was pretty, all right. This house could make you want things you never even knew about.

Scarlett clutched the plates and pizza crusts to her as she passed the open door. Except for the light from the television set the room was dark.

When she peeped inside she saw the sheriff stretched out on the couch, a box with the remains of the pizza on the floor, an open can of beans beside it. His arm, extended, dangled into space over a familiar black shape.

Scarlett stepped into the room.

"There you are," she whispered. She could hardly see the dog, but she heard the thump of Demon's tail. "What're you doing down here?"

Demon made a friendly groaning sound. The tail wagged again, sweeping pizza crusts over the rug. Scarlett stepped closer.

The sheriff looked more like a regular-type man now, rather than the police. Farrie was right: he was young and sort of good-looking. By the flickering light of the TV set she could tell he'd showered

47

because his hair was dried in little rattails over his forehead. He'd taken off the starchy tan uniform and wore jeans, and a plaid shirt that lay open and unbuttoned, exposing his bare chest. Where he had rolled up his sleeve his dangling forearm was solid, impressive, lightly spangled with hair. His feet, propped at the end of the couch, were bare.

Scarlett stepped over Demon to lean closer.

It wouldn't be so hard, Farrie had said. Scarlett was remembering the sheriff crouched in the driveway that afternoon with his pistol in both hands. *Big and tough, too,* her sister had pointed out. You needed that against Devil Anse.

But *married?*

Scarlett frowned. She supposed there were worse things. She wondered how old the sheriff was. If she had to guess she would say not much over thirty.

She bent over him. As he slept the dark fan of his eyelashes were noticeable, unexpectedly long and pretty. They were complemented by a straight sweep of nose, swollen at the tip where he'd fallen on it. His curved mouth, open, snored a little. Even unconscious he looked able to handle anything.

Scarlett felt torn. If she didn't look after Farrie nobody else would. Worse, they'd taken away her money at the Jackson County jail; they had nothing, now, to get them to Atlanta. She yawned suddenly, convulsively. It was just too much to worry about; she was almost asleep on her feet. She quickly straightened up, feeling a little too warm, strangely dizzy. It was the house. That furnace running like it would never shut off. It had nothing to do with looking at the young sheriff asleep on the couch half naked, in his bare feet.

"Let's go, Demon." She reached down to take the dog by the collar but it shifted away, pressing flat on the rug. "What's the matter with you?" Scarlett whispered. "You're not supposed to be down here."

Demon only hunched closer to the couch, lifting a massive head to lick the sheriff's suspended hand.

Scarlett stood watching. Mostly Demon stuck close to Farrie. On the other hand, she knew that the dog could act strange if someone was in trouble. Once Scarlett had fallen into a gully in the woods and hurt her leg and no one could find her. Demon had hung close as a leech that morning, not letting Scarlett out of her sight. And was sitting there, waiting, when some Scraggs cousins finally took the time to find her.

Before Scarlett could haul on Demon's collar the body on the couch stirred, and mumbled something. Demon promptly licked the sheriff's hand.

He seemed to flinch. "Dog . . . *out*," the sheriff muttered. "Damn . . . damn dog . . . mmph . . ."

Scarlett didn't wait for him to wake up. "Well, just stay there," she hissed. "I'll let Farrie take care of you in the morning."

She tiptoed toward the door. Demon was leaning against the sheriff's arm, staring at him adoringly. The dog had not even pricked up her ears at the mention of Farrie's name.

Scarlett made her way back down the hallway toward the foot of the stairs. There was no need to turn on the hall ceiling light, she thought, looking at its prisms winking softly; the sheriff was bound to wake up sooner or later and close up the house. A small noise made her look toward the etched glass panels that flanked the front door. What she saw made her catch her breath.

The porch light was on and the door was locked. But the face that looked at her through the decorated glass was what you would conjure up if you wanted to be scared half out of your wits—a wild, dirty gray beard, white-rimmed, burning eyes. A mouth grimacing now with words she could not hear.

Scarlett saw a grimy hand point downward, toward the lock. Then lift to jab at her.

She stood rooted to the spot, caught by those terrible eyes that bored into hers. *Unlock the door.* She could not hear Devil Anse's words, but she could see his lips move.

Never! If it had been a scream it would have burst out of her.

With her hand clamped over her mouth to keep from yelling, Scarlett turned and ran up the stairs.

Six

MADELYNE SMITH, BUCK'S SECRETARY, WAS filing some papers when he walked into his office. She turned from the file cabinet with a surprised flicker of her eyes as she took in the sheriff's muddy hat, paw prints across the front of his shirt, and coffee stains in a rather indelicate place on the front of his uniform trousers.

"My goodness, Sheriff," she said, "you sure wouldn't pass inspection this morning. You better not let your deputies see you."

At Buck's ferocious glare, Madelyne decided to leave it at that. Turning, she nearly fell over the Hound of the Baskervilles. She let out a shriek.

"Good grief, what do you call it?" Madelyne hastily retreated behind her desk. "Is it a dog or an animal Frankenstein?"

"I've had a bad morning," Buck growled. "It started early. Can you get somebody back in the communications room to turn down those damned Christmas carols?"

Deputy Moses Holt, hearing the commotion, came out of the hallway that led to the cell block. He stared at the dog. "Sheriff, I thought you decided we didn't have a budget for no K-Nine corps."

At the sound of his voice, Demon raised her black head and snarled softly. Deputy Holt went back inside the cell block and closed and locked the door. "Didn't mean no offense," he said through the bars.

"The dog's not a K-Nine," Buck explained tersely. He looked around for a good place to put the Scraggs dog but the cell block was already taken by his deputy. "It's a pet. You don't bother it, it won't bother you."

As Demon followed close on his heels into his office, Buck hoped he was right.

His secretary was not convinced. She stared at the massive animal that settled under Buck's desk, red tongue lolling out of its fanged mouth.

"That's the last thing I'd have for a pet," she observed. "What does it eat—truck bodies?"

Buck didn't answer. He was going through a stack of telephone messages. He was rarely late, and never had he gotten into the office with so much urgent business piled up and waiting for him. There were four or five calls from the volunteer director of the newly organized Committee for the Real Meaning of Christmas. So far the committee's nasty attitude on the subject of the cancellation of the Christmas living manger scene had made Buck wonder if they correctly understood the implications of their name. There was also a message in answer to a call Buck had left that morning before he left home:

the Methodist minister's wife, Grace Heamstead, had a houseful of company and couldn't come herself but would send her daughter Judith over with some clothes from the church's emergency clothes closet.

Buck put the note aside. He'd hoped Grace would come over with clothes for the Scraggs girls herself. It had seemed to him that a little finesse might be needed to get Scarlett and her sister into better, if nonetheless used clothing. There was something pathetically prideful in the two Scraggses that even Buck could see.

He picked up another memo, this one from his deputy sergeant in charge of state law-enforcement bureau liaison, reporting on the lack of information on thieves who were specializing in hijacking quarter-of-a-million-dollar tractor-trailer rigs in Jackson County.

If the sheriff's department didn't get something substantial pretty soon, Buck knew he was going to be inundated with inquiries from the Georgia Department of Criminal Investigation wanting to know details of the problem. Not to mention the considerable unhappiness already being heard from the local packinghouse and truckers.

Two refrigerated tractor-trailer rigs, one of them loaded with beef, had disappeared during December. The way the hijackers were operating, Buck had a feeling they would come back for at least another heist before they moved their operation elsewhere.

Convulsively, Buck yawned. Usually he didn't feel so bushed in the morning, but he hadn't slept well. He still didn't know what had prevailed upon him to spend the whole night on the couch downstairs with the television going. And early morning, with the knowledge that the two Scraggs females were in the house, had set him on edge. He'd showered in his mother's room, taking advantage of her private bath, but even so had been surprised by the strange child hobbling down the hallway with the giant dog when he sneaked back wearing only a towel.

That damned dog.

Buck shuffled through the piles of messages listlessly. The thing was called Demon, a fitting name if ever there was one. It had developed a neurotic fixation where he was concerned as it seldom let him out of its sight. He hadn't been able to get rid of the dog even during breakfast, when it kept licking his hand and leaning on his knees under the table. He'd had to finish his cereal standing up at the refrigerator, and he'd taken his cup of coffee out to the Blazer, intending to finish it on the way to work.

That had been a mistake.

The dog had followed him and when Buck locked the doors it jumped into the Blazer through an open window, knocking Buck's coffee all over his uniform. When he called the Scraggs females to haul it out, the dog had defied even them, baring its teeth and snarling when they tried to touch it.

"It's Demon's way of saying she don't want to," the gnomish child had explained blandly. "Sometimes she bites."

Buck wasn't going to put it to the test. On the

54

way down to the department he had considered opening the door and shoving the dog out into traffic, but attempted illegal disposal of animals was a punishable offense. He didn't feel like risking it, anyway; not as the county sheriff.

Now he stared at his telephone messages with a tired, unfocused gaze. He hoped he was never called upon to explain how he had been withstood by a mongrel beast that had refused to be evicted from a county law-enforcement vehicle.

"Buck," his secretary said, coming to the door of the inner office, "your telephone's ringing. Do you want me to take it?"

He shook his head. His telephone had been ringing for quite a while. Buck lifted it. "Grissom here," he intoned.

"Buck?" The voice was that of the bureau supervisor in the state criminal investigation department, Byron Turnipseed. "I hear you got a rash of truck hijackings in Jackson County. What's going on?"

"Just a moment." Buck reached down and lifted Demon's head from where it was resting burdensomely on his left knee. "Byron, yes, I've got problems," he said morosely. "Which one do you want to hear first? The separation-of-church-and-state injunction to mess up our Christmas pageant on the courthouse lawn we've had up here for about fifty years? The local nuts and their Committee for the Real Meaning of Christmas? Or a couple of"—Buck suddenly hesitated—"uh, runaways."

He'd decided at the last second not to describe Ancil Scraggs's granddaughters and how they happened to be spending Christmas with him. No one would understand, anyway. Not down in Atlanta.

The voice on the telephone quickly reminded Sheriff Grissom that the state's concern was not runaways but hijackers. Buck managed a weary smile. He didn't hear the rest as the voice in the telephone was drowned out by a series of disturbing sounds from the outer office.

Buck thought he heard his secretary, Madelyne Smith, uttering strange, shrill noises that were not at all like her usual conversation. Then he heard the deeper voice of the deputy, Moses Holt, saying something that sounded like: "Halt, hold it right there!"

At the same time, the big black dog under his desk came to life. Snarling and barking, it tried to squeeze past Buck's legs.

"Holy—" Buck grabbed at the edge of his desk so as not to be tipped out of his chair. "Hang on," he managed to say to Atlanta as, in the outer office, Madelyne Smith's voice hit a higher decibel.

The dog tangled for a brief second in Buck's telephone wire, then jerked the receiver out of his hand before breaking free. The criminal investigation department continued to talk as the receiver swung off the edge of the desk.

Buck was wearing his gun. As Demon barreled past him his chair went over, dumping Buck to the floor. He still managed to clap his hand over his service revolver. A reflex action, he realized moments later, that was eminently prudent. For looking over the edge of his desk, Sheriff Buck Grissom saw a tall, gaunt figure with a flowing beard and disordered gray hair standing in the doorway. Holding a twelve-gauge shotgun pointed straight at him.

Buck didn't need a description. It was Devil Anse. He was sure nobody else could look like that. From his position on the floor, the hardwood desk between them, it was clear they had the drop on each other.

"Sheriff," he could hear his deputy shouting, "we got a—a armed intruder!"

"Stay back!" Buck yelled in answer.

He could have used some help right then from the huge dog. Like having it charge Ancil Scraggs and disarm him. But the animal obviously knew shotguns, for it dropped to the floor and lay there on its stomach.

"Sheriff," Devil Anse said from the doorway, "I come about my female relations, Scarlett and Farrie, what is missing from home. I been told you got them somewheres around."

Buck lowered himself even more behind the desk so as to minimize a possible blast from the shotgun. From there he could see a stretch of green office carpeting and, in the doorway, a pair of ancient black boots. He considered a bullet in the old man's foot to disable him. He didn't think it would work. Not before his desk got blown apart by the twelve-gauge.

"They don't want to go home," Buck told him.

"Well, I don't doubt that," the voice of Devil Anse replied. "Scarlett's got a mind of her own, and the little one does what she tells her to. She ain't easy to live with, Scarlett ain't."

Buck was finding that out.

"I don't know what Scarlett told you," Devil Anse continued. "She can spin a mighty good story when she gets going. But I ain't about to force that girl to do nothing she don't want to."

Buck, recognizing a new element, thought that over and decided not to comment.

"No sirree," the grating voice of Scraggs went on, "I ain't going to trade Scarlett off to Loy Potter's boy for his new pickup truck. Not if I get a better offer."

Buck couldn't help it. He looked around the edge of the desk. "You *what?*"

"That's right, Sheriff." The old man stood leaning one shoulder against the doorjamb, shotgun now resting in the crook of his arm. The fierce, biblical prophet face, surrounded by dirty flowing gray hair, looked almost benign. "Scarlett's a rare piece," he said with relish. "Better looking than her maw before she ran off with that Tennessee guitar player." He paused. "Now, Sheriff, I allus look to where I can make a good trade, anybody who knows me will tell you that. And Scarlett needs a settlin' hand. Ain't nothing sinful—Potter's boy is willing to marry her."

Buck sat back on his heels. He couldn't believe what he was hearing. The old degenerate made it sound like he was trading off a hunting dog. Instead of a perfectly able-bodied—desirable—human being.

For a damned pickup truck.

"What about the little girl?" Buck said carefully.

"Farrie Fawcett?" The raspy voice turned ingratiating. "That's a delicate subject, Sheriff. She gets about funny on those skinny little legs, don't she? A

58

regular little hobgobler. I'd be willing to turn her over to the county, see what they could do for her."

Turn her over to the county? Buck choked down a surge of wrath. The cold-blooded old devil—the kid was his grandchild!

"Now Sheriff, let's do some straight talking." The voice in the doorway was sly. "In past days I have accommodated the law around heres to mutual benefit. Oh, not with your daddy, son—he was a man who shied away from anything that might even *look* like a purely good-hearted, generous gift with no strings attached."

Buck suddenly stood up, his gun leveled at Devil Anse's potbelly. "What's this about my dad?" he growled.

The old man looked surprised. "Lord, son, didn't I just say it ain't got nothing to do with yore daddy, may God rest his soul? We're talking about *you*. One thousand dollars, cash, and Scarlett's yours."

For a minute Buck was too stunned to speak. Then he felt a wash of red rage begin at his ears.

"Dirt cheap, too," the old man added sincerely. "Considering the good amount of cash young Potter said he would throw in on top of the ninety-three Dodge."

"You—" Buck began in a strangled voice.

His reaction plainly pleased Devil Anse.

"It's a bargain, ain't it?" The old man smiled a broken-toothed smile. "But Sheriff, I'm willing to make this sacrifice if it means a new, friendly feeling between this office and the Scraggs family business interests. I'll be honest with you, boy, since you took over from yore daddy it's been a real economic hardship for us in the Scraggs line of liquor services and auto parts supply. I want you to look at Scarlett as a public relations gesture of future goodwill and cooperation. On both sides."

"Your *family business interests*? Is that what you call them?" A pulse was pounding in Buck's head. *"Liquor services and auto parts supply?"*

"Son," Devil Anse said gently, "words like 'bootlegging' and 'car stealing' are out of date, don't you know that? Now Scarlett, if I tell her so, she'll stay with you. And mark my words, yore bound to get yore money's worth. No man's laid a hand on—"

"Money's worth?" Buck managed to bark. "You old viper! Are you trying to bribe a law-enforcement officer?"

He started around the desk, gun in hand. Devil Anse backed into the corridor.

"Sheriff, 'bribe' 's an ugly word," the old man protested. "I'd hoped not to hear words like that between us. Not about an honest little gift or two. The girl's staying at yore house, ain't she?"

Reluctantly, Buck stopped.

Devil Anse looked triumphant. "Didn't think I knew? Well, no telling what's already happened." He gave a truly repulsive wink. "Why don't you think of Scarlett as a—*trial offer?* Money back if you ain't satisfied, as they say on TV? You keep her a while, and if she don't give you—"

Buck was outraged by the sheer gall of the old man. He started for him. And tripped over Demon, who was under his feet.

"Dammit!" Buck exploded.

He staggered, stepped on the dog's tail, and to

the accompaniment of its anguished howls managed to reel forward and hit his shoulder on the door-jamb. But, thankfully, not his nose. In the outer office he could hear his deputy's warning shouts, Madelyne's shrieks.

When he looked up, the old man was gone.

Buck stood rubbing his shoulder, wondering if he had hit it hard enough to fracture it. He couldn't afford to be injured right now. Not with so much going on.

Worse, when he reviewed the conversation he'd just had with his visitor, he groaned. There was no doubt about it. Devil Anse Scraggs thought he had just made a deal.

Seven

FARRIE PATTED THE WHITE TURTLENECK top stretched across her stomach. "I can wear this with the red skirt over there, can't I, Scarlett?" she pleaded. "We wouldn't be taking too much."

Scarlett knew it wasn't a matter of taking too many of the church's clothes; it was simply that the top didn't fit. When the boxes had arrived Farrie had hopped like a small skinny bird from one to another, trying on everything. To judge from what the Methodist church had sent they hadn't expected someone her size. She *was* small for a nine-year-old. The minister's daughter, Judy Heamstead, had gone back out to the car for another load of donated clothing.

"Come over here," Scarlett told her. "Let's try on something else." She caught Farrie's arm before she could scuttle away, grabbed the white knit top and pulled it over her head, leaving her little sister in nothing but her ragged underpants.

Ordinarily yanking Farrie's clothes off like that

would have brought on a fit of outraged screeching, but this time she hardly noticed. Farrie was living in another world, so happy, so charged up about everything that Scarlett knew it couldn't last. She tossed the turtleneck into the pile of clothing that was rapidly becoming a small mountain on the Grissoms' dining room floor.

Scarlett hadn't mentioned Devil Anse's visit to Farrie but it weighed on her mind. Ever since their grandpa had showed up on the Grissoms' front porch wanting to get in, Scarlett had been unsure of how long they could really stay at the sheriff's house. Farrie might be convinced that the big tough sheriff could handle anything, but she wasn't so sure.

On the other hand, she told herself, Devil Anse might have come just to talk. If he'd come to take them away it could have been a whole lot different.

Still, she'd been jumpy as a cat all day long, thinking Devil Anse would come back at any minute. Or telephone. But nothing had happened.

"Oh, Scarlett, lookahere!" Farrie stepped into a pair of green corduroy overalls, hauling them up by the straps. The too-large pants almost swallowed her.

Scarlett sat back on her heels. The overalls had been made for somebody's fat little kid, younger than her sister; there was even a duck embroidered on the bib.

"You're supposed to wear a shirt with that," she said. "You can't go around with your bare shoulders and arms sticking out. Not in this weather."

From the look on her little sister's face nothing.

she could say would spoil her mood. They were surrounded by boxes from the church mixed with the Christmas decorations the sheriff's mother had left behind. Farrie had gone from one clothing box to the other like a whirlwind. Some of the clothes, Scarlett had to admit, were nice. Some looked almost brand-new.

"What's that?" With a cry, Farrie bent over a cardboard box to drag out a dress. When she held it up they could see it was a gown in a peach rayon satin, old, not in good condition. The sweetheart neckline was raveled and the taffeta flowers that decorated the skirt were so flattened that it was hard to tell at first what they were.

Scarlett frowned. "You don't need that. It looks like something yore grandma would wear."

Farrie pulled the dress over her head. The back gaped open where there were buttons she could not reach, and the squashed roses hung limply. As did the puffed sleeves. "Did you ever know my grandma?" She found a wide-brimmed straw hat with matching peach satin flowers and a huge bow in front with a rhinestone pin.

Farrie jammed it down over her ears. When she turned, arms held out, the ridiculous hat teetering, Scarlett had to smile.

"No, I never saw her." Scarlett had always wondered about the woman who'd been foolhardy enough to marry Devil Anse, but their grandma had died long ago and now no one ever spoke of her. "You better take that thing off. I don't know what it's supposed to be, probably somebody's old bridesmaid's dress."

Farrie came to stand in front of her. "What's a bridesmaid's dress?"

"You know what it is, we've seen 'em on TV." She cupped one of the fabric roses in her hand. It must have been pretty once: the inside was just like a real flower with little imitation white and green stalks. "Rich people have big weddings where all the bride's girlfriends dress up to be in the church with her when she gets married."

Farrie flopped down on the floor beside her. "Oh Scarlett, you could have that, a big wedding with bridesmaids and all, if you married the sheriff." She stroked a small hand down Scarlett's sleeve coaxingly. "You're so pretty, you'd make the best-looking bride."

Scarlett pulled Farrie's hand away. "I thought I told you to stop talking like that." Scarlett was wearing a black cotton shirt that Judy Heamstead had cinched with a leather belt with a big brass buckle, and a pair of tight but becoming jeans she'd found in the clothing boxes. The minister's daughter and Farrie hadn't stopped talking about how good she looked.

"Go help yourself to more clothes," Farrie urged. "There's lots left. Look at all the things I found."

Scarlett shook her head. She wasn't going to go hog-wild. Jeans and a couple of shirts and sweaters were enough. She didn't want to say it in front of Farrie, but she'd never liked wearing other people's clothes. Everyone had their dream; for Farrie, it was to live in a big house with a bed with a ruffled tester, and have a real family. For Scarlett, who had worn used clothing most of her life, it was to have her own clothes. Just a few. But all new.

Judy Heamstead came in carrying two cardboard boxes stacked on top of each other. "Here," she said, trying to see over them, "I hope these have got some shoes. These are sure heavy enough."

Seeing no place to put them, Judy opened her arms and let the boxes drop to the floor. The minister's daughter was seventeen and wore jeans with a huge oversized red sweater, a down jacket, and cowboy boots.

"Are you going to wear that?" She stared at Farrie openly. "My cousin Ina was a flower girl in that for my mamma's wedding years ago. The hat, too."

"A flower girl?" Farrie's eyes were big. "In a *real wedding?*"

"Take it off," Scarlett told her. Weddings were not a good subject. There was no need to encourage her sister. She got to her knees and pulled the boxes to her. "What I need for Farrie is a warm coat. What's in these?"

"I hope it's shoes." Judy sat down on the floor beside them. "You need shoes. You can't keep on those rubber sandals, it's too cold."

The minister's daughter stopped, her cheeks reddening. The reasons why the two Scraggs girls were at the sheriff's house were, her mother had warned, none of Judy's business. But since she'd brought in the boxes from the church, Judy had been dying to find out. "If these boxes don't have any shoes in them maybe we can find some of Sheila's old ones upstairs."

Scarlett was silent for a moment. "Do you know them? The sheriff? And his family here?"

The other girl nodded. "My mother and Alicia Grissom went to school together." She looked around the big room. "Mamma remembers when the first sheriff gave Buck's mother this house. It used to be in Mrs. Grissom's family but they ran out of money and lost it years ago. It was almost falling down. Hey, will you look here?" She seized something and held it up. "No wonder the box was so heavy! I thought there were shoes in it."

"Books." Scarlett picked one up, curious. "A *cookbook?*"

"It's stuff left over from the last rummage sale," Judy murmured. "Goodness, haven't you ever seen a cookbook?"

"No," Scarlett said. "We're Scraggses." Farrie lifted her head, listening. "If you don't know by now I better tell you. My little sister'n I are running away to Atlanta."

The look on Judy Heamstead's face was indescribable. "You're *running away?*"

Farrie opened her mouth to say something but Scarlett gave her a quick look. "There's nothing here in this town for us. Not for Scraggses."

"Oh, don't say that." Poor Judy looked nonplussed. "I'm sure there's—"

"Never mind, we're used to it, Farrie and me. That's why we're going to Atlanta. Can I"—Scarlett reached into the box again—"have some of these books?" She held one up. " *Five Hundred of the World's Best Potato Recipes.*' Can you learn to cook if you read it in a book?"

"Oh yes, that's what they're for. I don't really know what else is in there, people donated them." Judy's face was still crimson. "I don't like to cook much, myself."

"I love to cook. I just never saw any books that showed you how." Scarlett inspected a volume entitled *How to Have Fun with Your Wok*, and put it back. But she set aside an ancient copy of *The Fanny Farmer Boston Cookbook*, and *Prize-Winning Cakes and Other Desserts from Better Homes and Gardens*. "They got a real nice kitchen here," she said thoughtfully. "I saw it last night."

Judy jumped up with an expression of relief.

"Would you like to see the rest of the house? There's a tower room that's really neat. When my brothers and I used to visit Mrs. Grissom she let us play in it and make believe we were beautiful princesses waiting for a knight to come rescue us. Well, actually, the boys wanted it to be World War Two and we were being attacked by Nazis."

"A tower?" Farrie said eagerly.

Scarlett frowned. "We better not."

Farrie was already on her feet. The two girls started for the hall, Judy explaining to Farrie about the original Blankenship house that had stood there, and the Union cavalry raid that had swept down out of Chattanooga in 1863 and into the Nancyville valley.

"The Yankees burned the front part of the house," she was saying enthusiastically. "So when the war was over Mr. Blankenship opened the cotton mill and made a lot of money and had the house rebuilt the way you see it now. That's when the front porch was put on, and the tower."

Upstairs, Judy threw open the door to their room.

"This was Sheila's." She gestured as though they hadn't already slept there. "Don't you just love that bed? I always wanted one like it. Sheila's daddy the old sheriff gave it to her on her twelfth birthday." She turned and started down the hall again. "Mrs. Blankenship used to sew a lot when Sheila went away to college. She used the tower for a sewing room. It has the neatest window where you can look down the side of the mountain and see all of Nancyville."

They came to the end of the hall up the stairs and the door to the tower room. Judy tried the doorknob. "Oh drat, it's locked." Her face fell, disappointed. "I guess we'll have to wait and get the key from Buck."

"No we won't." Farrie bent to press her eye against the keyhole. "It's just a ole-fashioned spring lock, no tumblers or nothing like that. I need a pin." She straightened up and took off the big hat.

"We don't need to do that," Scarlett said quickly.

"Good golly, can she really do it?" Judy's eyes had grown rounder. "Open a locked door?"

"Well," Farrie said, "for a lock with tumblers I need a little knife." She had taken the rhinestone pin off the front of the wedding hat. "But a pin will do for this old spring lock. I can hot-wire cars, too." She bent to the door, the opened pin in her hand. "I can open the door on a ninety-three Coupe de Ville and get inside in no time. I got a uncle, Lyndon

Baines Scraggs, who showed me how to do car locks. But I'm way faster now than he is."

At that moment the door clicked and swung open. Farrie stepped back, grinning. "See? I told you it wasn't no big thing."

The Victorian turret room was cold. Storage boxes were stacked against the walls and a dressmaker's dummy stood by the window. Scarlett shied at it. "What's *that?*"

"I guess that's Sheila's dress form," Judy told her. "Sheila's mother sewed for her all the time she was in college. Sheila always had the prettiest clothes! She was Homecoming Queen, and Rush Week Queen, and Harvest Ball Queen—Mrs. Grissom was always making her some kind of evening dress, Sheila never wore the same one twice."

Scarlett stood in front of the dummy, fascinated. Here, in this house, people not only learned to cook out of books but they sewed, too. And according to Judy never wore the same clothes twice.

"C'mon," Judy said, brushing past her, "let's open the window."

They threw up the sash and a blast of frigid air rushed in. Scarlett crowded into the bay. They hung out over the sill, the shingles of the roof just below.

"Look!" Farrie cried.

The Grissoms' house stood on the western side of Makim's Mountain overlooking the Nancyville valley. The mountainside fell away sharply. Faint snow drifted in the bitter air, frosting the oaks and pine trees and the roofs of houses farther down. In spite of the snowfall they could still see the town, the spires of churches, the trees on the courthouse lawn.

"That's where they're going to have the living Christmas tree," Judy said, pointing. "My mom and dad have been working on it for two weeks, getting people to volunteer."

"Living Christmas tree?" Farrie's breath was like smoke in the cold air. She hung into space and Scarlett took a firm grip on the back of the peach satin dress.

"Used to be the Living Christmas Pageant," Judy explained. "One year I was a shepherd, and you freeze to death not moving at all while people drive by in their cars. We used to have a contest every year for the Best Baby Jesus, but babies could only stay out fifteen minutes at a time unless it was pretty warm at Christmas like it was last year. When Jason Ellison won his mother wanted to use an electric blanket but Susan Huddleston, the county welfare worker, said that fifteen minutes was still the limit."

Scarlett knew who Susan Huddleston was. "What happened to the Baby Jesus this year?"

"He got eliminated." Judy shrugged. "The government said we were breaking the law holding a religious spectacle on county property. So this year we have to have something non—*nonspectaclarian*."

Judy thought it over, frowning. "Anyway, Mr. Ravenwood, who teaches the high school chorus, said we could have a Living Christmas Tree." She leaned out to point. "Down there next to the courthouse in all those trees. If you look real hard you can just see where they're building it."

"I can't see anything." Farrie followed the pointing finger. "What is it?"

"I just told you, *the Living Christmas Tree*. It's a big

wooden thing shaped like a Christmas tree. And when you look at the back of it there's steps and places for people to stand on. We haven't had a rehearsal yet but Mr. Ravenwood says that you stand on your part of the steps and you're holding candles in both hands. That's the living Christmas tree part. People are supposed to be living Christmas tree decorations."

Farrie made a sound of sheer awe.

"And you sing," Judy added, "Christmas carols. The whole tree is singing and people drive by and see that."

Scarlett looked at her. "Singing?"

"It's a sort of Christmas concert. There are a lot of people that are still mad about the Best Baby Jesus contest, though." Her face brightened as she pulled back inside. "You're going to stay here with the sheriff until after Christmas, aren't you?"

Scarlett hesitated, aware that Farrie was looking at her pleadingly. "Well," she said slowly, "unless something changes."

"Oh, I don't think anything's going to change, according to what my mother said. That means you can volunteer for the Living Christmas Tree. All you need to do is stand there and sing." Judy Heamstead saw the look on Scarlett's face. "You can sing, can't you?"

Scarlett was trying to think of something to say.

"Yeah," she said finally. She was feeling like she was throwing away the last chance they had, and helpless to do anything about it. "*Farrie* can sure sing."

Eight

"TRIPPED OVER THE DOG, DID YOU?" DR. Halliwell asked. "I bet that's the first time old Devil Anse got away because a lawman fell over a pet. How're you with cats?"

"Doc, look," Buck began.

"That's a pretty interesting animal." The doctor looked over his glasses at Demon's vast length stretched out on his office carpet, her paws crossed over her muzzle. "I've never seen one quite like it. 'Course, as you know, Yorkshire terriers are my passion, the wife's, too. However, I saw a Neopolitan mastiff one year at the Atlanta Dog Show," he said, looking reminiscent. "Biggest damned thing I ever did—"

"Doc," Buck interrupted forcefully, "if you like dogs you can have this thing." He struggled to his feet, favoring his swollen right arm and hand. "In fact, the way things stand right now, I'll do pretty nearly anything to get rid of it. It's developed some sort of obsession about sticking close to me—you

75

won't believe this but it even follows me into the men's room and stands there, watching. It's driving me nuts!"

"Sit back and calm down," the doctor told him. He reached over and took Buck's nose between thumb and forefinger and moved it slightly. "I feel a little play in the cartilege there. Want me to stabilize that nose with an adhesive strip?"

Buck pulled back quickly. "Hell no, I don't need my nose taped up! I'm not exactly looking like a role model for the department as it is."

Dr. Halliwell raised his eyebrows. "Have it your way. But we're not fooling around here, Buck. Just because I popped that shoulder back in the socket doesn't mean you don't have to take care of it. I want you to keep the arm in a sling for the next ten days." At Sheriff Grissom's audible groan he went on: "Except, of course, you can take it off when you go to bed."

"I can't keep my arm in a sling," Buck protested, "not for ten days! Look at me. A banged-up nose, my right arm useless, and I'm busier'n hell this time of the year what with hijackers and the crazy business about no Christmas pageant on the courthouse lawn—"

"If you'd wanted a pet," the doctor interrupted, "I could have fixed you up with a nice Yorkie male pup. Six weeks old, papers, and all shots. My wife's little bitch just had a fine litter."

"Pet?" Buck turned to glare at the dog on the office carpet. "That thing's no damned pet. It acts like it's going to tear your throat out if you try to make it do something it doesn't want to do."

At the sound of Buck's voice, Demon lifted her head, wagged her tail, and gave a soft, loving moan.

"Looks pretty friendly to me." The doctor leaned over and slipped a blue and white canvas sling over Buck's head. "Don't turn down a trusting animal's love," he advised as he guided Buck's hand through the opening. "Believe me, the wholehearted devotion of a dog is one of the few genuine gifts a man gets in this corrupt and unhappy world. Nelly and I wouldn't give a million dollars for our family of Yorkies."

Buck lurched to his feet. As he did so, Demon got up from the floor and with its huge tail wagging swept a stack of medical magazines from the doctor's desk.

"You see what I mean?" Buck reached for his wide-brimmed sheriff's hat with his left hand. "It eats my lunch, I can't get a sandwich halfway to my mouth before it gulps it down, Saran Wrap and all. Then it leans all over me when I'm trying to drive, and if I try to shove it out of the Blazer it acts like it's going to take my hand off." He twisted his elbow unhappily, looking down at the sling. "I don't know if I can take this for ten days," he said, turning to go. "I've got to take it off sometime. This is my gun arm."

"Suit yourself, boy," Dr. Halliwell called after him. "But that shoulder's not going to get better unless you give it a rest."

Giving it a rest, Buck found as he made his way out to the clinic parking lot, was easier said than done. And getting into the Blazer with only one hand was a challenge. Once inside the dog hunkered up next to him and rested her big head on his right shoulder, making Buck yelp in sudden pain. The fact that he was backing out as this happened, the steering wheel held only by his usable hand, made the Blazer veer in the same direction. With the result that the vehicle narrowly missed scraping the length of Dr. Halliwell's Fleetwood Cadillac parked next to it.

Buck sat muttering under his breath, not only from the sharp twinge in his shoulder, but from the disaster that had almost overtaken him. Dr. Jerry Halliwell loved his brand-new 1994 Fleetwood Caddie almost as much as he loved his Yorkies.

Buck slipped his arm out of the blue and white canvas, gritting his teeth against the pain. He had thought to experiment with driving without the sling, but he'd promptly put it back on when he saw his hand, his fingers the color of smoked sausages.

It was going to be some holiday.

"Sit down over *there*," Buck snarled at the dog. For once it obeyed, moving to its side of the front seat, looking at him reproachfully.

It was beginning to rain as they took the highway back to town, another sleety assault from the mountains to the north that made the road treacherous, especially driving with one hand. Buck had to hook his right elbow against the steering wheel to help turn it.

Both sides of the road were lined with the brightly colored local product: handmade chenille bedspreads now flapping in the wind. Making chenille bedcoverings had been a cottage industry for decades in the Georgia mountains. Most of the families along State Road 12 made money in the summer and fall when the tourists were around. Now it looked as though they were trying for some Christmas money.

In spite of bad weather, the clotheslines were hung with spreads with designs of peacocks, Florida flamingos and palm trees, and in honor of the season, outsized chenille Santa Clauses.

The Last Supper bedspread, Buck was relieved to see, was not as popular as it once had been. The local God-fearing mountain people had never seen anything objectionable in rendering Jesus and his disciples for sale in cotton tufts in primary colors. But the thought of actually sleeping under one of the Last Supper bedspreads, Buck had always felt, was more than a little daunting.

The radio suddenly came on. "Sheriff," the county police dispatcher said, "can you pick up?"

Buck propped his elbow on the steering wheel to hold it and lifted the receiver. "Yeah, George."

"Do you," the dispatcher wanted to know, "care to answer a call from the Committee for the Real Meaning of Christmas? The chairman, Junior Whitford, has been calling you again about the music. He says the committee ain't approving 'Santa Claus Is Comin' to Town' for the Living Christmas Tree to sing as it celebrates a pagan ritual."

At that moment the Blazer entered Nancyville's downtown. There were only a few shoppers on Main Street and they hurried along under umbrellas. Overhead, the whirling aluminum garlands said Joyous Noel, and Happy New Year.

Buck was suddenly reminded that he didn't have a date for New Year's Eve. Didn't, actually, have any place to go. In years past he had always dated Susan Huddleston, and Susan had made the arrangements. Now he found the prospect of an unplanned New Year's Eve surprisingly depressing.

He clicked on the Blazer's radio. "I must have been celebrating pagan rituals all my life," he told the dispatcher, "because I've been singing 'Santa Claus Is Comin' to Town' since I was in kindergarten. The head Druid, Mrs. Brown, taught it to all of us."

Buck, too busy maneuvering the Blazer to get more than a glimpse of the wooden structure in front of the courthouse, was reminded that Cyrus Ravenwood, the high school band teacher, had guaranteed the Living Christmas Tree was the answer to their problems: a totally secular entertainment that had been successful in other places faced with similar court orders.

Buck hoped Ravenwood knew what he was doing. But he had his doubts. Right now even "Santa Claus Is Comin' to Town" was under fire.

"George, have we heard from any truckers?" He didn't want to forget about their major problem. The department was averaging one call a day from local truckers asking what they were doing about the hijackings.

"All quiet so far," the radio told him. "You got a call from Inspector Byron Turnipseed at the Georgia CID, that's all."

Buck signed off. The state's criminal investigation department could wait until tomorrow; any help Byron Turnipseed offered with their hijackings was limited by a skimpy state budget. Small north Georgia counties' law-enforcement departments usually had to shift for themselves.

Following that line of thought, he remembered the Scraggs sisters. For the first time he felt what could only be a rush of reluctant sympathy for Devil Anse's offspring. The old outlaw came rightly by his name. Who else but a devil would think of selling off—there was no other word for it—his own flesh and blood? "Free trial offer" be damned!

Then there was the strange little elvish child. There was no telling what was wrong with her, a variety of birth defects, probably, from the look of it. The kid needed medical attention. Probably for the first time in her life.

And the other one. Scarlett.

Instead of coherent thoughts a series of fleeting images raced through Buck's head. The screaming hoyden in the dirty pink underwear panties Moses Holt had dragged across the floor of the jail, yelling her defiance. Scarlett standing with her arms wrapped tightly around her in his mother's driveway, black hair streaming in the wind. A few minutes later holding her sister in her arms and stroking the child's hair, her face transformed with tenderness.

Buck stopped in the middle of his thoughts, astonished that he was even thinking about Scarlett O'Hara Scraggs. As an antidote he quickly tried to picture Susan Huddleston.

He couldn't.

Buck pulled into the driveway and cut the Blazer's

engine, having to cross over the steering wheel with the wrong hand to reach the key. He sat there regarding his home for a long moment, a faint frown between his eyes.

He had no idea why he had been fantasizing about Devil Anse's long-legged brat; the old man had put the idea into his head with his free trial offer, damn him. And for all her rough upbringing, Miss Scarlett O. Scraggs was fantastically tempting.

Buck got out of the Blazer. The cold wind almost blew him onto the front porch. Once inside, the warmth of the house enveloped him, along with strong tantalizing odors. He remembered he hadn't made any arrangements about what they were going to have for dinner. His stomach rebelled at the thought of another pizza.

He started down the long hallway, stopping abruptly at the light coming from the parlor.

He stepped inside. There stood the big blue spruce Christmas tree, fully decorated. The strings of Christmas tree lights that embraced it sparkled and blinked.

It was the first time in years that Buck had seen a Christmas tree with seemingly every last one of his mother's collection of ornaments on it, including the paper garlands he and his sister had made in the first and second grade.

With all the stuff on it the tree should have been a mess. Instead, every branch, almost every needle, was so covered with decoration that the great blue spruce tree radiated a remarkably homey, jumbled sort of—well, beauty.

If you were familiar with the Grissom family ornaments you could just stand and look at the tree for hours, he thought, remembering the story behind each item fashioned by children's hands, each faintly crazed old glass ball, the grandparents' German imported Father Christmases holding their blown-glass miniature trees, the now less-than-sparkling gold and silver tinsel ropes that came from the long-closed Nancyville McCrory's.

Someone had done a good job. With the strings of lights, the tree blazed happily.

At that moment the damnedest, most bizarre apparition appeared from around the other side of the tree. Startled, Buck could only blink.

It seemed to be some sort of lumpy pink satin specter, drooping around the bottom, wearing a flappy straw hat with satin flowers.

When it saw him standing there the banshee recoiled in horror. Then it whirled, scuttling for the dining room with faint, ratlike squeaks of alarm.

Buck stared after it. The little sister? Then what the hell was she doing dressed up like Halloween? He started after her.

The odors in the far end of the hall were even more tantalizing. Before Buck could throw open the kitchen door, though, it swung out and some strange girl—woman—stood in the door with the kitchen light behind her. A ravishing female in a dark shirt, tight jeans, her dark hair pulled back with a ribbon.

"Hel-lo," Buck said. He stepped back in appreciative surprise.

It was undoubtedly somebody who'd come with

Judy Heamstead to bring the church clothes. But new in town, Buck had never seen her before.

"Don't be down on Farrie," the willowy figure cried. "She didn't mean any harm to the tree, she just wanted to fix it up. She's never seen anything like it before!"

For a moment he stood staring. "Farrie? *Farrie?*"

Even in the glaring kitchen light he couldn't believe it. It *was*, he realized with a sinking feeling, Scarlett O'Hara Scraggs.

"It will be all right," she was telling him rapidly. "You'll feel better about it when I feed you dinner!"

Dinner? In a daze Buck gazed past her. If the Christmas tree wasn't, by some miracle, a mess, the kitchen certainly was. Everything seemed to have been pulled out from where it belonged and then emptied, dropped, or spilled in a different place. Still, when he sniffed the air it smelled wonderful.

Buck's moment of hope vanished with Scarlett's next words.

She touched him on the arm, gazing up at him somewhat anxiously. "Don't look like that," she murmured in her husky voice. "You're gonna like it. I cooked every bit myself."

Nine

"THE GIRL FROM THE CHURCH SHOWED me how to get the meat out of the freezer and thaw it," Scarlett said. "That was the biggest part of the job."

They were seated, Scarlett and Farrie and Buck, at the big mahogany table in the dining room. Through the sliding doors the Victorian parlor looked better without the clutter of cardboard boxes. The bright glitter of the huge Christmas tree reached almost to the ceiling.

"I was supposed to put the meat in the microwave thing, but she'd left by that time and I couldn't get it to work. Anyway," Scarlett added, looking down at the assortment of food on the table, "ten pounds of hamburger is a lot. When I got it thawed out I knew I was just going to have to keep cooking."

"No problem." Sheriff Buck tried awkwardly for a piece of meatloaf with the fork in his left hand. "I can't get over it. Everything's so delicious."

The meatloaf slipped and landed on the tablecloth beside his plate. Scarlett tactfully picked it up and put it on her own. She'd been watching the sheriff closely from the moment they'd sat down, but he seemed sincere. Of course he'd been a little surprised that she'd cooked dinner, even after Scarlett had explained that she'd learned it all from the cookbooks they'd taken from the clothes boxes that afternoon. He'd looked tired when he came in and Scarlett saw at once he was out of sorts: Demon had left her marks all over his uniform, and he'd had some sort of accident as his arm was in a sling. Sheriff Buck went right into the dining room, pulled up a chair, and sat down.

Now, Scarlett saw, he'd certainly been hungry in spite of his hurt arm. He'd had a helping of the Italian spaghetti with meat sauce, two big servings of Spicy Shepherds' Pie, a slice of House and Garden's Heirloom Recipe Meatloaf, and a cup of homemade chili. That left only the Swedish meatballs to go.

Farrie, too, hadn't taken her eyes off him. Scarlett picked up the bowl of meatballs and shook her head at her sister in warning. She knew Farrie wasn't thinking about whether or not the sheriff liked the food.

Marriage. That was the only thing on Farrie's mind. It was right there in her face. Sooner or later Sheriff Buck Grissom was going to wonder why her little sister kept staring at him like that.

"Take off your hat," Scarlett told Farrie, frowning. "People don't eat dinner with their hats on."

Without shifting her gaze, Farrie reached up and pulled off the hat with the rhinestone pin and peach satin roses. The sheriff wasn't watching; he was having trouble with the bowl of meatballs. The brown, glistening globes in what the cookbook described as authentic Swedish gravy kept bouncing away from his probing fork. He wasn't at all good at using his left hand; the tablecloth around his dinner plate was spattered with food.

Scarlett picked up her own fork. "Here, let me," she said.

He started to object, then watched as she scooped a serving of meatballs and gravy onto his plate. "The dinner is delicious," he said with an effort, "I'm not kidding. I can't believe you taught yourself to cook like this out of a book." He looked down the table, hesitating. "You don't have any— ah, vegetables, do you?"

Scarlett was cutting a meatball in half for him, and stopped abruptly. "Vegetables? I just cooked up all the meat, I didn't think about any vegetables! What kind of vegetables do you want?"

"We have iced tea," Farrie piped.

The sheriff looked across the table, his eyes resting on the too-big dress that hung drooping around the child's arms and neck. "Does she have to wear that thing?" he growled.

Scarlett studied her sister. "That's the first pretty dress Farrie's ever had. If it bothers you, I can take it away later on when she goes to bed."

Buck leaned over his plate. "Damned if I can make up my mind, everything is good. But what I had before is, I swear, the best chili I've ever tasted."

Scarlett held out her fork to him with a piece of meatball on it.

"I like to cook," she said simply. "I already know how, a little. But it was better to find a book with those things in it since I had to use up all that hamburger."

He studied the fork. "I'm not doing very well, am I?"

"There's a lot on the table," she admitted.

Slowly, the sheriff opened his mouth and Scarlett popped a piece of meatball into it.

It was a perfectly ordinary thing to do, to offer to help him eat when he couldn't use his right hand. But Scarlett was suddenly and strangely aware they were close enough so that she was looking right at the sheriff's long eyelashes. Which curled up and were a dark red color, like his hair. His eyes were bright blue. Up close Buck Grissom had creamy smooth skin. She was particularly struck by his mouth: wide and full, with something downright attractive about it even as he chewed the meatball.

Across the table she knew Farrie wasn't missing a thing. But Scarlett couldn't tear her eyes away.

Never in her life had she been so close to a man and so mindful of how good-looking he was. And how warm, she thought with a sudden gulp, and how big!

Sitting there, Scarlett felt a fascinated rush of excitement from the top of her head down to her feet. She could hardly move.

At that moment the sheriff looked up, expecting another meatball. And their eyes met.

There was a strange silence.

Scarlett sucked in her breath. Good Lord, from

the way his eyes widened, and he sort of stiffened, she could tell that he felt it, too!

They just sat staring at each other. Finally Buck said, his eyes never moving, "You don't have to feed me."

Scarlett still held up the empty fork, forgotten. "I don't mind," she whispered. "I like looking after people."

"I can see that." He had a peculiar expression on his face.

"Why," Farrie said loudly, "don't you feed him some meatloaf?"

They both jumped.

"Well," Farrie explained, "he didn't hardly get to eat any of his own meatloaf. It kept falling on the table."

A scowl settled on Buck's face. He looked around, seemed to shake himself, then lurched abruptly to his feet.

"Dinner was fine," he announced hurriedly. "I enjoyed it very much. Right now I think I'll go make myself some coffee."

He crossed the dining room, and at the door he turned.

"I've got some paperwork to do, I'll be in the den." He looked everywhere but at Scarlett. "You two can just watch television or whatever it is you want to do."

After Buck had left, Scarlett and Farrie sat for a few minutes in silence.

Finally Scarlett said, "You can help me clean away these plates and take them into the kitchen."

Farrie got up from the table. "We don't have to wash them, Scarlett. They got a dishwasher in there."

Something inside Scarlett snapped. She didn't know what had brought on her sudden bad mood, but it was certainly there.

"Yes indeed, Miss Smarty, and if you know how to work a dishwasher you can just go right ahead and do it!" She picked up Buck's plate and scraped what was left of the meatballs and shepherd's pie onto hers. "Otherwise you can come on with me and I'll wash, and you wipe, and try not to break any of this good china."

Farrie had listened with an open mouth. Now she put the big hat with the roses back on. Under it, she pouted.

Scarlett decided to ignore her.

It was late when they got the kitchen cleaned up. When she began dinner Scarlett had found everything she needed, but after washing the dishes she was not so sure how to put it all back. It was not easy in the Grissoms' big, fancy kitchen with built-in cabinets, two pantries, convection oven, the microwave, and assorted appliances.

When they were through, Farrie wanted to go into the Victorian parlor and sit under the Christmas tree rather than go upstairs and watch the television in the sister's room. Somewhat reluctantly, Scarlett gave in.

The big high-ceilinged parlor was so bright with the Christmas tree that they didn't bother to turn on other lights. After some trial and error Scarlett figured out how to turn on the radio in the stereo console. She sat down beside Farrie on the floor.

Since Christmas was only a few days away the local radio station played mostly Christmas carols. In alternate strings the red, green, blue, and white lights on the tree blinked on and off.

Outside it was sleeting again. Icy rain threw itself up against the glass of the parlor windows with a faint hissing sound. When the furnace cut on it added its warm, muted *whooosh*.

Farrie leaned forward, hugging her knees, her pixie face lit by the flashing lights of the tree. Scarlett was glad her little sister wasn't trying to talk about anything. Everything that Farrie wanted to say was in the air anyway.

Scarlett stared up at the big tree remembering one particular year they'd had to leave Catfish Holler at just about Christmastime for some reason that no one ever explained, but probably because the law was after the Scraggses. With two of the Scraggs uncles they'd gone over the mountains into North Carolina to stay a week in a motel. It was a bad place. The rooms in the old cabins looked clean but stank so much they could hardly breathe.

On top of everything else the motel had been full of hookers. When their uncle Lyndon Baines Scraggs wasn't around to keep an eye on things, Scarlett sat in the middle of the motel bed and held Farrie in her arms, listening to the loud music, the doors slamming until almost morning. Scarlett had been about fourteen then. She hadn't been able to show her face outside their room for truckers chasing her, wanting to give her money for what they thought she was selling.

No, Scarlett thought as she studied the back of her head, Farrie didn't have to say a word. She could almost hear her say: *We could stay here, Scarlett. It's up to you.*

Scarlett bit her lip. It was true she would do almost anything for Farrie. It had been that way ever since her sister was born. But nobody could ever accuse Scarlett O'Hara of being talked into a crazy idea; she was too smart and stubborn for that.

She leaned forward, clasping her own knees in her arms. It was pretty cold-blooded to consider marrying someone just to have a roof over their heads. The only trouble was, when she was around the sheriff she didn't feel very *cold-blooded* at all.

She shut her eyes for a moment. Mercy, just thinking about Sheriff Buck's curly eyelashes, wide mouth, and determined chin filled her with the strangest feelings! When Scarlett opened her eyes Farrie was studying her. Why did her sister always have to look as though she could practically read her mind?

"He likes you, too," Farrie told her. "You could see it when you were feeding him meatloaf."

"Meatballs," Scarlett said. "Not meatloaf."

Farrie waited.

"All right," Scarlett said, frowning, "just don't harp on it. I'll see what I can do."

When Buck came out of the den at eleven the Christmas tree lights in the parlor had been turned off. It was quiet, no interminable Christmas carols from Nancyville's AM radio station, no female voices. No giggling. They'd finally gone to bed, he told himself.

As he always did before he turned in, Buck bolted the downstairs doors and turned the furnace thermostat to sixty-five degrees. By the time he'd got upstairs the house had already begun to cool.

The sheets were fairly cold when he climbed into what was, he'd always been told, his maternal grandfather Blankenship's Lincoln-style bed. It took a moment for Buck's body heat to warm it up. That gave him plenty of time to lie in the dark and listen to the wind pound the sleet against the northeast side of the house with a hiss like the sea hitting the shore. Then the wind, moaning in a low, wintry voice.

God help those without shelter on a night like this, both man and beast. That was what his dad, Sheriff Buck Grissom, Sr., always said.

Around the holidays Jackson County had the homeless coming over the mountains on the interstates from cities like Nashville. Sometimes there was a problem with families sleeping in cars or in old pickup trucks. On a night as cold as this it could be dangerous to pull off the highway to some supermarket parking lot to sleep. Half the homeless heading south for Atlanta or Florida didn't have warm clothes, much less blankets. Buck thought about getting up and calling the jail, checking to see if anybody'd been brought in.

In the next instant he rejected the idea. There was a directive out to the department about taking the homeless to shelter; he'd written it himself back before Thanksgiving. The night shift could handle it, Buck told himself. No need to jump out of a warm bed as his dad always had to check on every little thing downtown.

Buck turned over on his side and shut his eyes. He didn't want to think about the homeless, he didn't want to think of vagrants out in a night of wind and bitter cold. Nor the condition of the Scraggs sisters when he'd brought them home: Scarlett in rubber sandals and a thin cotton dress, the younger one not much better off in sneakers and an old discarded football jacket. Old Devil Anse made money from his rackets; there was no excuse for anyone bringing up their own kin like that.

Cursing his need to get some sleep, Buck flopped over on his opposite side. And suddenly jerked up in bed holding his bad shoulder.

"Confound it," he yelled. His mistreated arm throbbed painfully. He considered getting out of bed and putting the sling back on. Only briefly.

Gritting his teeth, Buck slid back down in the bed again. With his left hand he carefully pulled the covers up to his chin and closed his eyes. He kept his eyes closed determinedly as the wind lifted something loose outside the house and banged it across the lawn. A shutter thumped loudly. Or it was the unknown thing again, making an extended trip across the frozen grass outside. Buck told himself he wasn't going to get up.

Somehow, even with all his fretting, he managed to drift off to sleep. Unfortunately, he had one of the worst dreams of his life.

He was dancing, and Buck was no dancer, at a

wedding reception where half the guests were troll-like children running around wearing hideous peach satin dresses with big, floppy hats.

Even asleep, Buck cursed.

Then he discovered he was holding in his arms one of the most enchanting women he'd ever seen. The motion of the dance wafted her long dark hair out into the air like silken smoke. Her eyes were the same mysterious hue. And her lips—ah, her lips! That warm, full mouth was made for kissing. Buck was aware he hung over her, hopelessly fascinated, and that she wore a distinctive perfume. Aroma of meatloaf.

Buck looked down and could see she was wearing a costume in a vaguely antique style. The upper part of her gown exposed a good bit of her truly dazzling, pushed-up breasts. There were diamonds at her throat, and at her ears. On her head he saw, amazed, a diamond tiara. She gave him an impish smile.

In spite of the dazzling enchantment Buck was wary. There was something about the whole thing—

Abruptly he looked down again, and his suspicions were confirmed. He was Prince Charming, all right: he had on his best uniform with all his ribbon decorations and awards, including Georgia State Lawman of the Year, his Sam Browne belt, and even his motorcycle police boots, shined like mirrors. And somehow while dancing he was managing to hold his wide-brimmed hat in his uninjured hand.

The only trouble with Cinderella and Prince Charming was that Buck knew all too well who Cinderella really was. Awake or asleep she was beginning to haunt him, the most tantalizing, puzzling, desirable female he had ever known. But he knew in his heart that didn't make it right. She was still Devil Anse's granddaughter.

Besides, at any moment the clock would strike midnight and the whole thing would turn upside down.

Cinderella put her hand on his arm and said something Buck couldn't quite make out. Sure enough, the clock was striking. He noticed now his bad arm was in a sling.

"Be careful," Buck started to say.

Instead, she twined herself around him. The music grew faster. They spun with it. Buck couldn't break away. She pressed against him so tightly his shoulder was in agony.

"Ow!" Buck yelled, becoming fully awake.

He still couldn't move. The same body held him down in the bed, and hands—a mouth—were on his face. His bad arm was caught in between, shooting arrows of pain up into his collarbone. With an oath Buck flailed both arms, disregarding the agony, and flung himself out of bed, dragging the leechlike body with him.

"Wait!" Scarlett O'Hara Scraggs cried. "I'm just tryin' to make it easier! For both of us!"

Buck staggered to the bedside lamp, hauling her with him. He turned it on.

"Easier?" He tried to pry her arms from around his neck, aware as he did so that her warm, slightly struggling body was pressed intimately against his pajama front. "What do you mean," he bellowed, "easier for *both* of us?"

He had no idea what she was talking about. The only thing that was plain was that the Scraggs girl was trying to assault him in his own bedroom. Had tried, actually, to crawl in bed with him.

"Yes." Those luminous dark eyes were right in his. Her grip was surprisingly strong; he still hadn't been able to get her hands unclasped from around his neck. "I'm gonna give you what you want," she whispered huskily.

Without warning Scarlett Scraggs stood on tiptoe, strained upward, and glued her mouth against Buck's.

His first impulse was to wrench her away from him using whatever force necessary. But then, as those indescribably soft and tempting lips pressed against his, Buck found his vision fogging. The room seemed to slowly revolve. Sensation became so heated that the knifelike pain in his arm and shoulder faded completely away.

Reluctantly, his own arms went around her.

"Scarlett," he murmured, knowing he was a damned fool but not able to summon enough willpower to do much about it, "open your mouth."

She did. Wide open.

"Not like that, sweetheart." He put his thumb under the tip of her chin to gently close it. "Let's try this again."

Even as he spoke a small voice in the back of his mind warned him that Scarlett's actual words were that she was going to give him what he wanted.

Buck had no idea what he wanted at that moment, except the impossible.

He was lost. So drowned in the sexy, tender warmth of Devil Anse's granddaughter that his mouth gently explored her lips and felt them open to him. It was a long time before Buck drew back. After that memorable kiss, Scarlett's look was as dreamily unfocused as his.

He suddenly had a terrible suspicion. "Scarlett," Buck said hoarsely, "have you ever been kissed before?"

He could see the answer in her face.

Scarlett Scraggs stood before him in a nightshirt with a faded Atlanta Braves logo on it, evidently something from the church's used-clothing boxes, her beautiful young breasts thrusting up under the cloth temptingly. Around her ravishing face her dark curls were tumbled and mussed, her mouth slightly swollen with kissing. She looked ravishing. It was more than Buck could stand.

Somewhat roughly, he took her by the hand and pulled her to the door.

"Whatever this is all about," Buck found himself saying, "it'll have to wait until morning. We'll thrash it out then."

She pulled back from him. "I don't want to wait until morning. We gotta—"

"It will wait," Buck barked, "oh, yes it will!" He needed to get her out of there.

But she grabbed the doorjamb with both hands. "Don't put me out yet! I need to talk to you!"

He pried her fingers loose. "You've got to go, Scarlett." God knows there was regret in his heart.

"I'm sorry, but my—uh, bedroom is no place for you right now."

She tried to fling herself at him again. "Well then, why can't you kiss me one more time?" Those gorgeous dark eyes flashed up at him. "You can do that much, can't you?"

"Not on your life!"

He pushed Scarlett O'Hara Scraggs out into the hall, and shut the door. He was, he realized, shaking.

Buck started for bed, then thought better of it, and returned to the door. And locked it.

Ten

THE NEXT MORNING THE WEATHER OVER the Blue Ridge mountains had cleared, but it was still cold, and the wind blew. Someone on the lower branches of the Living Christmas Tree lost their music to a sudden gust and sheets fluttered away across the courthouse lawn like a flock of winter birds. A burst of laughter broke up the chorus of "The Wassailing Song" and the singers straggled to a stop.

"All right, all right," Mr. Ravenwood, the Nancyville high school bandmaster shouted. "Let's hold it down."

Some of the children who were too small to be a part of the tree were sent to chase the music. Scarlett wrapped her free arm around the wooden bar that held up her part of the scaffolding and shivered so hard that it made the boards shake.

Beside her, Farrie said, "What's the matter?"

"Nothing. I'm just cold, that's all."

Her little sister's expression said that Scarlett should have worn the good corduroy coat she'd gotten from Judy Heamstead's church clothing boxes instead of just a light denim jacket. Everyone on the tree or down below among the parked cars was huddled in parkas or down-filled ski coats.

Farrie herself looked like a different child in a blue and white windbreaker, a knitted cap with a big white pompom, and matching blue mittens. Her eyes blazed with excitement, and her cheeks, red with the cold, looked as though someone had painted them. But then Farrie had been singing, Scarlett told herself. Anytime Farrie could sing she was happy.

"What's going on? Who's doing that up there?" Mr. Ravenwood had come close to the tree. "Stop it! You're making the whole thing shake."

Scarlett ducked her head. The last thing she wanted was to attract attention. Earlier, when they had arrived with Judy Heamstead and her mother, the band teacher had wanted to know if he hadn't seen Scarlett somewhere before.

She'd wanted to take Farrie and go back to the sheriff's house right then. If word got around that they were runaway Scraggses, Scarlett knew, it would be all over. But instead Judy had grabbed Scarlett and Farrie and pushed them toward the tree. "All you have to do is sing," the minister's daughter told them. "Nobody's going to know who you are, and if they do, they won't think anything about it. My dad is in charge, anyway."

Mr. Ravenwood was seeing that the music was returned to their proper owners. "Page three, everybody. 'Here We Come A-Wassailing.' From the top."

Scarlett peered at her sheets. Judy Heamstead

had just explained to her what "wassailing" meant. Scarlett had never seen the word before in her life.

All the songs for the Living Christmas Tree had been carefully chosen, as they were not supposed to sing about anything that dealt with what Mr. Junior Whitford and the rest of the committee considered to be the Real Meaning of Christmas. That was too bad, as it eliminated just about all the carols any of them had ever heard.

After running through what was left, Christmas was sort of watered down. Although the song they'd just sung, "Here We Come A-Wassailing," was a lot better than "Frosty the Snowman" or "Santa Claus Is Comin' to Town." The same thing went for "I Saw Mommy Kissing Santa Claus." She saw Farrie's face scrunch up when Mr. Ravenwood asked them to turn to it. Kissing Santa Claus was nothing to sing about for someone whose mother had been fooling around—maybe not with Santa Claus, but a Nashville guitar player—one Christmastime.

> "Here we come a-wassailing
> Among the leaves so green—
> Here we come a-wandering
> So—faaiir—to be seen—"

Farrie's clear voice rose over all the singers, even the Methodist and Baptist church choirs singing down in front. Farrie had a big voice for such a little girl; most people didn't believe it until they heard her sing. Scarlett saw her sister holding the music sheets up in front of her, but she wasn't following them, she was looking over the courthouse lawn as though expecting someone.

> "Love and joy come to you
> And to you, your wassail too
> And God bless you and
> Send you a Happy New Year—"

Scarlett couldn't help thinking there wasn't much for Farrie to hope for if she was looking for Sheriff Buck Grissom. They'd hardly seen him the past two days. He'd brought Scarlett some groceries, but the only one who'd really seen him for more than a brief moment at morning and night was Demon. The dog went to work with him during the day and hung around when he was doing paperwork at night or watching television in the den. Not, they all knew, that Buck was crazy about having Demon around: he'd tried to shut Demon up in the bathroom that morning so he could slip off to work. But they'd all seen what Demon had done to the bathroom door before he let her out.

> "Love and joy come to you
> And to your wassail, too—"

Scarlett lost her place in the music and stopped. She didn't have the heart to tell Farrie what had happened in Sheriff Buck's bedroom two nights ago. She didn't understand it herself.

Scarlett knew she hadn't exactly laid the groundwork for the sheriff's marriage proposal, but what she'd done should have worked. After all, what did

Reese Potter want with her, if not that? According to Reese and Loy Potter, it was worth Reese's brand-new pickup truck, which they'd offered Devil Anse.

Buck Grissom was different, she knew now. In his room he'd acted as though he were feeling the same strange, exciting things as Scarlett.

Inwardly, she sighed. That kiss had opened a whole new world. Then something had happened. Right in the middle of the best part, when he was breathing hard and looking into her eyes and there seemed to be a pocket of fire about to burst right between them, Buck had pushed her out the door and locked it!

Since then he hadn't spoken two words to her.

"All right, cut! *Cut!*" the music teacher shouted down below. "We're not getting anyplace with that one. Let's try something else."

Scarlett leaned up against the wooden bar and rubbed her cold nose. The Living Christmas Tree was scheduled to sing every night at dusk on the courthouse lawn during the last five days before Christmas. Topmost position on the tree was going to be the Spirit of Mistletoe, who had a solo that was still to be announced. On the rest of the tree Bells and Angels stood on alternate rows, the "candles" the Angels were going to hold in their hands actually flashlights so the ever-present wind from Makim's Mountain wouldn't bother them.

She had to stop thinking about Buck Grissom, Scarlett told herself. Nobody wanted the sheriff to show up and hang around for the rehearsal and take them back to his house any more than she did. But it wasn't going to happen.

Mr. Ravenwood was wagging his arms up and down. "I've got to get to the bottom of this." He looked up to the tier of Angels. "You up there," he said, pointing. "How long have you been singing contralto?"

It was a minute before Scarlett realized he meant Farrie. Heart pounding, Scarlett stuck her head through the plyboard and looked down. "She doesn't know what that means," she called. Neither did she.

The band teacher took off his John Deere cap and ran a hand through his hair. "Make her come down here."

It took Farrie a moment to climb down, Scarlett right behind her. As soon as everybody found out they were Scraggses they were going to start for the sheriff's house. Even if they had to walk the whole way.

"She has a tremendous, powerful voice," a Bell was saying. "Little girl, where's your mother?"

An Angel came up to stand beside them. "I think they're the Heamsteads' houseguests."

The director studied Farrie. "Sing 'I Heard the Bells on Christmas Day.'" He handed her a sheet of music so she could follow the words. "Not all of it— just a couple of lines."

Scarlett stepped back. The choirs were crowding around Farrie and she knew what was going to happen. Just as soon as her sister started to sing they would ask a lot of questions. She saw Farrie with both feet planted firmly, ready to open her mouth, and thought that she never looked more like a bushy-haired, snub-nosed pixie, her black eyes gleaming.

> "I heard the bells on Christmas Day,
> Their old familiar carols play—"

After the first words bystanders were exclaiming. Scarlett backed away even more. Farrie could sing, there was no doubt about that. She just had to find a way to get both of them out of there when she stopped.

Judy Heamstead had followed her. "Where are you going, Scarlett? Mr. Ravenwood's excited about your sister's singing. Aren't you going to listen?"

Scarlett sidled across the courthouse lawn toward the parking lot. "I've heard Farrie plenty of times. Listen, are you'n your mother going home anytime soon?"

"In just a few minutes. Scarlett, what's the matter with you?"

Scarlett shook her head and kept going.

There was no need to hang around. She shouldn't have let Judy and her mother talk them into singing on the Living Christmas Tree. It was not where Scraggses belonged.

Neither, Scarlett told herself as she turned to look back at the courthouse, was learning to cook out of cookbooks, or dressing up in other people's clothes. Fish out of water. That's all they'd been all along.

After the fussing over Farrie's singing died down people would only make fun of her. It was time they gave up all this foolishness and left Nancyville.

In the parking lot Scarlett leaned against the Heamsteads' car to wait. She didn't see until the last moment the tall dark shape that suddenly loomed up at her.

Scarlett's heart leaped. Maybe Buck was meeting her like this! Maybe they could get the misunderstanding between them straightened out.

'Maybe he'd hold her in his arms and kiss her again, she thought hopefully.

"Well, Scarlett girl," the tall shadow said, "looks like you've fixed yourself up real good."

Scarlett whirled to run, but Devil Anse grabbed her. She looked beyond him to the crowd on the courthouse lawn, wanting to yell for help but knowing it wouldn't do any good.

"Farrie and I don't have anything to do with you anymore!" she burst out.

"Now listen here, Scarlett." He gave her arm a shake. "I got something mighty important for you to do and I don't want no messin' up, y'hear me?"

When she didn't speak, Devil Anse nodded. "That's right, listen good, girl. Me'n Sheriff Buck Grissom's got a agreement, the first time we managed to get such a thing for our Scraggs business. That's something to brag on, seeing how his daddy wouldn't never listen to no talk. Every time the old sheriff saw me he'd start shooting up everything for a mile and a half with that sawed-off shotgun he used to carry. I never could get one word in edgewise. But the boy's different. I allus said young Grissom's reasonable."

Scarlett stared at him. "What did you do?" she cried.

Someone backed their car out down the parking lot. It started toward them. Devil Anse pulled her behind a car.

"Ain't nothing permanent, yet," he growled in Scarlett's ear, "it's in the nature of a free trial offer. But I figure the way things are going yore young sheriff won't waste too much time."

Scarlett pulled back to look up into his face. "Grandpa, you tell me what you done!"

He gave her arm a cruel twist.

"Ain't what I done, girl, it's what I want *you* to do. Now, when you've made young Buck happy, you just deliver a little message for me. Tell him in view of all I have done and am going to do for him, I want him to just stay at home, rest up, and not worry about any hijackings."

Scarlett managed to wrench her arm away. "When I have made him *happy?*" The full meaning was just sinking in. "You mean—"

When he nodded, she yelled, "I won't do it!"

"Won't do it?" The shaggy white brows came together. "Scarlett, don't talk to yore old grandpa like that. Didn't I let you have that puny baby sister of yourn to play with, when she's never going to be no good except taking up space and eating food what should go to the able-bodied? You got a durn sight better treatment, girl, than you deserve, all things considered."

With a sob, Scarlett lunged away from him. "You leave us alone," she cried. "You've never done anything for Farrie and me—except make us a part of the Scraggses!"

The car that was on its way out of the parking lot

slowed, looking Scarlett over. When she didn't seem to want any help, it went on.

Scarlett's mind was racing. Devil Anse had made some sort of offer to Buck Grissom. She still didn't believe it. Her heart was being torn out of her to realize that it was all just a free trial offer. To see if Sheriff Buck liked it.

Now, she thought, he was probably trying to make up his mind!

She circled away, blindly bumping into parked cars. Her grandfather followed. "Are you listening to me, young lady? I don't want to have to put up with no foolishness from you. You please Sheriff Buck just as hard as you can or you'll have to explain to me why you didn't. Do y'hear me?"

Scarlett broke into a run. They were going to have to leave for sure now. Buck Grissom would never tell Scarlett the things she wanted to hear now. Devil Anse had made that plain.

They wouldn't even stay for the Living Christmas Tree, she thought, fighting back tears. That was out of the question with Devil Anse lurking around every corner, telling her what he wanted her to do.

They had to leave Nancyville just as quick as they could. The only thing was, Scarlett dreaded telling her little sister the reason why.

Eleven

"THIS HAS GOT TO BE A CASE OF THE world's meanest people," Officer Kevin Black Badger said, "to hijack a truckload of Christmas turkeys. The birds were going up to the state school for the deaf for Christmas dinner. The place is mostly kids, too."

Buck followed his deputy down the shoulder of U.S. Route 29 as passing traffic thundered by. "Watch the dog," Black Badger reminded.

Buck gave him an irritable look. "Don't worry, I'm not lucky enough to have the damned thing run over."

They stopped at a place where the grass of the shoulder had been chewed into strips. "This was where," Black Badger said, pointing to the tire tracks, "the Piedmont Poultry driver pulled his rig over to check his brakes. He hadn't even put out his flares when this pickup truck comes roaring along, pulls up beside him, and two guys hop out and hit him over the head. When the driver came to last night he was lying here in the freezing rain, and his eighteen-wheeler was long gone."

Buck bent, hands braced on knees, to look at the truck's tire tracks where they reentered the highway. Somehow he had hoped he'd seen the last of the hijackers, that they'd moved on to greener territory up in North Carolina or Tennessee. But it looked like that wasn't going to happen.

In any event, the theft of a truckload of Christmas turkeys meant they would shortly have a message from Byron Walker at the Georgia State criminal investigation department. And if the truck was headed north over the state line, as Buck suspected, that could even bring in the Feds.

He realized his holiday was looking even bleaker, when he hadn't thought that was possible.

"It still had a full load when it left," Kevin Black Badger was saying. The deputy was a Native American from the Cherokee reservation in the Smokies and prided himself on his tracking, both animal and vehicular. "You can see by the depth of the tire imprints that it was still loaded up." He hesitated, frowning. "Turkeys are not something you can get rid of like cigarettes, or sides of beef, Buck. My guess is they must be going to sell them out of the back of the truck."

Buck straightened up. "Good work, Kevin." There was nothing else he could say. He only wished that the big Indian could do some tracking wizardry and follow the hijacked truck down miles of concrete to its final destination.

That, Buck told himself, only happened in movies.

"Write it up," he told Kevin. "Have you got anything on the pickup truck the hijackers were riding in?"

Demon sat leaning against the deputy's leg, making affectionate, whimpering noises. Black Badger bent to pat her head. "It's pretty standard Sears Roebuck tread, but I've been checking it out for idiosyncracies."

"Good." Buck started back toward the Blazer. "Keep at it and let me know."

As Demon followed him the other man called out, "That's a nice dog you've got, Sheriff, she'd make a good bear hunter. Let me know if you ever want to sell her."

Buck would have sold the Scraggs dog on the spot if he thought he could get away with it. Now the animal rushed past him in spite of his shouts, leaped through the open window on the passenger side with a great flailing of legs and claws and damage to the Blazer's paint, and threw itself down in the seat.

Muttering under his breath, Buck eased himself into the Blazer. He considered taking his arm out of the sling, but a few minutes driving without it coming down had proved what the doctor had said: the arm needed a rest. When it didn't get it, it hurt like hell.

Buck shifted gears carefully with his left hand and pulled the Blazer out onto the highway. It was not easy going even with two working hands; they were in the high Blue Ridge where the grades were steep, slippery, and filled with early traffic. The black ribbon of the road slashed through second-growth forest and on both sides rose green-black mountain pines, bare thickets of oaks and beeches. The woods had taken over the mountains after more than a century and a half of not-too-successful farming; down the road in the back country there were people who still lived in cabins and cooked on wood stoves and ate by the light of kerosene lanterns. And where deer, wild pigs, and bear were still hunted by the inhabitants, in or out of season. Protected by law or not.

And, Buck was suddenly reminded, up there somewhere in a hollow that lawmen, including his late father, had yet to locate, was the kingfish of all southern Appalachian outlaws, Mr. Ancil Scraggs. And all his thieving, conniving, alcohol-tax-evading, breaking-and-entering, grand-theft-auto, assault-with-a-deadly-weapon kin.

Except for two.

Reluctantly, Buck's thoughts went to Scarlett O'Hara Scraggs. That black-eyed, long-legged vision that flitted distractingly through his mind when he least wanted her to.

What in the devil, he wondered, had prevailed upon her to practically attack him night before last? Some sort of backwoods experiment? If so, it had been unnerving, plus he hadn't been able to stop thinking about it and that worried him.

When he'd been engaged to Susan, Buck told himself irritably, she'd never preyed on his mind like that. On the contrary, theirs was a rational, well-adjusted relationship.

On the other hand, Scarlett Scraggs was a mental toothache, one that wouldn't leave him alone, lovely and troubling and presumably innocent enough so that you had to wonder how she'd managed even to exist in the Scraggses' degenerate, criminal environment. Of course she'd been dedicated to bringing up the strange little sister. That had isolated both of them to some extent, he supposed.

What, he suddenly asked himself, was he going to do about Scarlett Scraggs? He'd gotten to the point where he couldn't imagine turning her and her sister over to Susan Huddleston after the holidays and just walking away, never to find out what had become of them.

As a law-enforcement officer, Buck's professional detachment was second nature. These two, he told himself, were just strays. Runaways. A case for the county and the state social services.

But, the other part of Buck's mind argued, Scarlett O'Hara Scraggs was different. All you had to do was see her in those jeans, properly cleaned up, with a ribbon in her hair, to know *how* different.

Dammit, if they ever *did* get to Atlanta he knew what would become of them; any cop could read you that scenario. The sleazeballs told girls who looked like Scarlett that they could get them into modeling school where they could make lots of money. Only there was no modeling school.

Buck carefully steered the Blazer onto a side road, the short cut into Nancyville. Some idiot, he saw in the rearview mirror, was riding his bumper, indifferent to the sheriff's-department insignia on the Blazer and the telltale police radio antenna.

He still had to make one stop at the office for a

meeting with a Hare Krishna delegation from Atlanta who wanted to talk to the sheriff about alternate forms of winter-solstice celebrations. Buck intended to listen to them but politely turn them down. Then he was going to take the afternoon off and go home.

He found he was looking forward to it. He had to fight down the anticipation of delectable odors of cooking in the house, wondering what Scarlett had fixed. It was the pits, as he had found out last night, to get a McDonald's hamburger and fries and eat it alone in the den in front of the television when there were better things to be had in the kitchen.

Tonight, Buck promised himself, he would sit down to dinner with Scarlett and Farrie. What had happened the other night was best forgotten—a mistake, that was all. God only knows he wished he could forget the look on Scarlett's face when she asked him if he could kiss her again. Just thinking about it made his body ache. He was going to have to keep that under control, too.

The 1993 Dodge pickup behind him pulled out as if to pass and then suddenly dropped back, neatly sideswiping the Blazer's bumper.

Buck stared into the rearview mirror, amazed. Was there somebody in Jackson County who had a perverted desire to spend the rest of the year in jail? The way this idiot was driving it looked like it!

Gingerly, favoring his right arm, Buck pulled the Blazer to the edge of the road and slowed down to give the jackass the benefit of the doubt and let him get by. After all, he thought a little self-righteously, it was the holiday season.

The police radio suddenly came on.

"Sheriff," the dispatcher's voice said, "I got a message from a Mr. Rama Rasmurtha McNally of the Hare Krishnas that they're running a little late for your meeting."

"Cancel it," Buck told him curtly. The pickup truck had made another dive at the Blazer's front fender. He couldn't believe it, but it was trying to run him off the road. "Right now I haven't got time for any more holiday freaks."

The pickup dropped back in another sideswipe. There was a metallic tearing sound. The Blazer lurched wildly. Buck seized the steering wheel with both hands. That hurt like hell; he suppressed an anguished yelp.

"Sheriff?" the dispatcher said.

Buck looked in the side mirror.

The blue pickup was accelerating in the left lane. Coming back again. Through the Dodge's windshield he could see a wild-eyed, contorted face under a cowboy hat.

Buck cursed.

What had old Ancil Scraggs said about trading off for a '93 Dodge pickup? Some redneck moron named—something. Potter?

Buck gave the side mirror a savage glance. The Dodge pickup gladiator looked as though he were dumb enough to have a name like Potter. Like one of the shiftless Potter clan that ran a service station over White Creek Gap.

The idea that Devil Anse would try to give his own granddaughter to some cretin like the one trying to smash in the Blazer filled Buck with fury.

Forgetting his sore shoulder, he jerked the van into the path of the truck as it came on again.

The two vehicles, both doing about fifty miles an hour on the narrow road, collided with an earsplitting clang. Snarling with pain and temper, Buck spun the Blazer's wheel left again. The Blazer creamed the pickup a second time.

Zigzagging, the truck went out of control and ran off the road on the far side. Buck slammed on the brakes. Before he could get the Blazer turned around, working furiously even with his arm in the sling, the blue pickup backed up, turned with tires skidding, and roared off in the opposite direction.

On the radio, his dispatcher was practically yelling for instructions. Buck fumbled the receiver to his shoulder with his throbbing right hand.

Demon, who had been crouched beside him through the whole thing, now leaned out the window barking wildly at the retreating pickup.

"Shut up!" Buck shouted. He pressed the button to talk. "Yeah, George, I'm okay. I just need an APB on a ninety-three Dodge pickup. License number—"

Hell, with everything going on he hadn't gotten the license number!

"Pickup's license number unknown," he said. "But I would like to talk, in the worst kind of way, to the scrawny snotnose wearing a cowboy hat who was driving it. See what you can do."

The idiot tried to kill me, he thought, signing off. It damned sure wasn't anything else.

Anger pounded in his head. Now that he'd gotten a look at Scarlett Scraggs's would-be bridegroom he had to wonder just how innocent she was after all.

Having the side of the Blazer smashed in didn't exactly put him in the most tolerant mood.

Buck stepped on the gas, feeling justifiably raw. By damn, he had a few questions he wanted to ask!

It took only a few minutes to whip through downtown and head for home. Buck had canceled the meeting with the Hare Krishnas through his dispatcher; there was no reason to stop at the office.

As he turned off the road into the driveway he drove through a spot of chill winter fog, then pulled the Blazer up to the front door. He watched while the dog vaulted out of the front seat and ran up on the porch.

Buck moved more slowly, taking time to circle the Blazer and assess the damage. He swore under his breath. He only hoped the pickup was just as banged up, because the department couldn't afford the bodywork this was going to cost.

He mounted the front steps, favoring his aching right arm. Once inside the downstairs hallway, a smell of something heavenly greeted him.

Buck missed his mother's presence in the house, her bustle of pre-Christmas activities with church and her friends, the amount of holiday baking she still managed to do. But miraculously, he saw, something just as good had come to take its place.

There was the odor of simmering, roasting, delectable food in the air. He sniffed, then drew in a long breath. He was practically frozen from standing out on U.S. 29 examining tire tracks. The warmth of the old house enveloped him, and the radio in the kitchen was playing. Buck made out the local station's nonstop program of Christmas carols, not the secular stuff the Living Christmas Tree was struggling with, but regular old-fashioned carols. Someone was singing "O Holy Night."

He started down the front hall. The door to the parlor was open. Inside, the tree, lights winking, stretched to the high ceiling.

He paused in the doorway to admire it. A beautiful tree, he thought somewhat grudgingly, even loaded down with all the Grissom family junk.

The dog scrambled down the hall ahead of him and Buck followed it. The old-fashioned swinging door to the kitchen opened to his push and he found the place blazing with lights. Something was boiling and steaming away on the stove. The first thing Buck saw was that the old wooden kitchen table was covered with more food than he'd seen in his life.

It seemed to be all vegetables. Dinner, fixed early.

There were casseroles of what looked like broccoli with melted cheese, and glass baking dishes with what appeared to be onions baked with a crusty cheese top. There were rows of baked potatoes in their skins decorated with bacon pieces and creamed spinach. Then grilled tomatoes, and more cheese. Whipped potatoes with lightly broiled, fluffy tops, french fries beside them. There were braised carrots and candied carrots, a dish of candied yams. A bowl of green peas mixed with slivers of mushrooms. Garbanzo beans with onions and tomatoes.

Buck's eyes began to glaze over. Obviously Scarlett O'Hara Scraggs had been raiding the freezer again. He turned to look for her and found her there, sitting at the end of the table, her bent head propped in her hands. When she looked up he saw she'd been crying.

"Farrie's gone," she said tonelessly.

Twelve

"WHAT DO YOU MEAN, SHE'S GONE?" BUCK said.

The girl before him held her head in her hands. "Farrie's never done this before." Her voice was rough with tears. "Ever since she was born, practically, my little sister's never gotten mad with me. And she's never, never run off."

Buck looked around. The kitchen was littered with dirty dishes and pots and pans. Scarlett Scraggs was not a neat and orderly cook. After a moment's hesitation he drew up a chair and cleared a space between the platter of french fries and the garbanzo beans with tomatoes.

"Scarlett, let's take this from the beginning." He couldn't help noticing that in spite of her air of misery, she was wearing her dark hair pulled back with a blue ribbon again and looked adorable. "We're talking about your sister Farrie?"

She nodded, eyes downcast.

Buck had come into the kitchen wanting an explanation. After all, some Scraggs-appointed boy-friend had tried to kill him. Now, at the sight of Scarlett's tear-stained face, he found all he wanted to do was take her in his arms and comfort her, kiss that luscious, downturned mouth, the tousled gypsy hair. It was a feeling that slightly amazed him.

He cleared his throat. "Your little sister's gone somewhere," he said, "without telling you?"

She shook her head. "Not 'gone somewhere,'" she corrected him, "she's *run away*." Her voice dropped even lower. "Farrie hates me."

He found that hard to believe. Not the way Scarlett hovered over her. Besides, the goblin child couldn't have gone far; it was raining.

"Hates you? How could anybody hate you, Scarlett? Didn't you say you've practically dedicated your life to her? What did you fight about?"

Her eyes slid away. "It was just something to do about us. Talking about where we belong."

He was seeing Scarlett O'Hara Scraggs being devious. Buck wondered what they had really talked about. He opened his mouth to find out more but the wall telephone in the kitchen rang. With a groan, he got up to answer it.

Scarlett lifted her head to watch Buck lean up against the kitchen wall with his head bent, frowning, as the voice on the other end said something at length.

Buck Grissom was young, but you could just tell by looking at him how powerful he was as sheriff; people jumped when he spoke. And he nearly always scared Farrie half to death. He was a big man, crisp and neat in his tan uniform. His shoulders stretched his shirt tight, and below, his trousers stretched just as tightly across his muscular backside.

It had taken a lot out of Scarlett to explain to Farrie about Devil Anse, how he wanted Scarlett to be friendly with Buck Grissom the way he'd wanted her to be with Loy Potter's son. Only this time it wasn't just a '93 customized six-cylinder Dodge pickup Devil Anse was aiming for, but the sheriff himself.

In return for doing what he said, Devil Anse expected to get a lot, like the sheriff's looking the other way as far as Scraggs family businesses were concerned.

Watching Buck now, Scarlett couldn't help wondering if Buck had made up his mind about Devil Anse's offer. He was hunched against the wall, his hand on the back of his neck, rubbing it as he talked. For a moment she almost felt dizzy. Why not, a little devil in her head whispered, pick up from where they had left off? That is, letting him kiss her?

She was so taken with this idea that she jumped when Buck suddenly roared: "Television crew? George, are these people out of their minds?"

Scarlett's heated, forbidden thoughts faded and she gave herself a shake. What she had told her little sister was right, that in the end what Devil Anse wanted her to do would bring only trouble not only to Buck Grissom, but to all of them. The only thing to do was leave Nancyville. Since the sheriff's department still had their money they would have to hitchhike, and even Scarlett didn't like to think about how they would manage.

When she'd told all this to Farrie, her sister cried, "Sheriff Buck wasn't being good to us just because of Grandpa's idea—he *likes* you, Scarlett! He doesn't act like Devil Anse!"

"Well, he's thinking about it." Even while she said it Scarlett remembered his arms tight around her, the strange mystery of his kiss. "Grandpa made his offer, and he says Buck's thinking it over."

Farrie had jumped to her feet. "I don't care what you say, we're not leaving! I won't listen to you! Mr. Ravenwood told me I'm going to be the Spirit of Mistletoe on the Living Christmas Tree, I'm going to sing a part all by myself!"

Farrie was working herself up to be sick, Scarlett knew. She reached out for her, but her sister backed away.

"We *can't* leave!" Farrie wailed. "Do like Devil Anse says, Scarlett! If the sheriff wants you to be nice to him—*do* it!"

Scarlett's mouth fell open in surprise. But before she could stop her, Farrie had stormed out of the kitchen.

In the upstairs hall she leaned over the banister to yell, "If you make me leave, Scarlett, you'll be sorry!"

It was what children always said, Scarlett told herself, when they were mad. She left it at that and went back to her cooking. All afternoon she'd thought Farrie was in the front part of the house, sitting by the tree she'd finished decorating, watching the lights.

But when Scarlett looked for her some time later, Farrie was gone.

Buck hung up the telephone. "We've got to hurry, if we're going to look for your sister," he told her.

What he didn't say was that in just a few short minutes, according to the department dispatcher, the delegation of Hare Krishnas along with a television news crew from an Atlanta television station would be arriving at the house.

According to George the dispatcher, Nancyville's mayor and city council members had ducked a confrontation at the courthouse that afternoon. When the Atlanta television news crew wanted to know who enforced the ruling about religious displays on county property the answer had been: the sheriff. It had only taken them seconds to pile into their cars and start for Makim's Mountain.

"Come on, hurry!" Buck pushed Scarlett toward the kitchen door. When the television people arrived he had to have both Scraggs sisters accounted for, but preferably not hanging around where anyone would notice them. It wasn't every north Georgia sheriff who had a resident sexpot in the house. And a child he couldn't reasonably explain.

First they had to locate Farrie. "Let's start upstairs," Buck said.

Scarlett didn't resist as he hurried her down the hall. "You're looking for clues," she said breathlessly.

"Yeah, clues."

The truth was, Buck didn't have a clear idea of what he was going to do. He had only a few minutes left before the media arrived and he was no expert on missing kids; little Farrie could be any-where.

Upstairs, he dragged Scarlett to his sister's old bedroom and threw open the door. But when Buck saw what was on the bed, he swore.

The new clothes, or at least new to the youngest Scraggs, were laid out neatly on top of the ruffled bedspread: a blue and white windbreaker, a knitted cap with a big white pompom, a pair of mittens. Even a peach satin outfit and oversized hat that looked familiar.

Scarlett picked up the hat and held it to her, looking stricken. "When I went to look for Farrie, I saw she'd left all her clothes here. She didn't even take her warm church coat."

Buck had a sinking feeling. This much he did know about runaways: they frequently left things behind as a kind of message. And the one from Far-rah Fawcett Scraggs said just what it looked like. *Good-bye.*

He couldn't bring himself to look at Scarlett. It was bad enough to search for a runaway in summer or spring when the weather was good; a night out in the open then was not exactly fatal. But this was a child who had a hard time taking care of herself even in the best of circumstances. Now it was win-ter in the mountains with a cold rain falling and night coming on.

So were the Hare Krishnas, Buck thought grimly. And the Atlanta television crew.

Somehow, he told himself as he picked up the telephone on the night table by the bed, he was going have to get through this and make it right. If he didn't, he might be the first Grissom to leave the profession of law enforcement in the three generations since Grissoms had been Jackson County sheriffs.

He rang his office direct. Madelyne Smith had already gone home, but Moses Holt was still there.

"Mose," Buck said, "I need some help right away." He watched Scarlett, her head bent, stroking the roses on the big floppy hat. "I need an expert tracker. We may have a lost child. I want you to find Deputy Kevin Black Badger and send him out to the house."

Thirteen

THE VAN ROLLED INTO THE CIRCULAR drive before the Grissom house and came to a stop. It waited a moment for the two automobiles behind it to come up, and then the van's door opened. A tall figure, dressed in a saffron robe, cardigan sweater, and sandals wet from the steady rainfall, got out. He was followed by a woman also wearing saffron robes and carrying a drum, and another Hare Krishna, a short man who opened an umbrella. Both men had shaved, uncovered heads.

Buck was standing on the front porch waiting for them. He said, "Okay, let's hold it right there."

The television van from Channel 10 in Atlanta sped up the drive, swerved around the other vehicles and pulled up on the grass right in front of Buck, coming to a stop over the spot where he knew his mother had her bed of early daffodils. A man with a television camera on his shoulder jumped out and aimed it at Buck.

"Excuse me, Sheriff," someone called, "but could

we have a shot of you talking to the alternative-program people?"

Buck felt the back of his neck tighten. He had already discarded the sling on his arm, aware that "I fell over a dog" did not project the best image for a county sheriff. His arm throbbed painfully. In spite of it, he stuck both thumbs into his Sam Brown belt.

"If there's an alternative program I don't know anything about it," he said sternly. "And if there is such a thing, it's not in my jurisdiction."

At the same time Buck was a little nervous about Scarlett Scraggs; it was almost as if he could feel her eyes on his back. He had asked her to stay out of sight until he could get rid of the delegation and the media, his excuse being that he wanted to get to work quickly afterward and organize a search for the little sister.

That, he told himself, was only the truth.

"But Sheriff, you're going to be down there tomorrow night," the TV cameraman said, his camera right in Buck's face. "To make sure the local committee for the Real Meaning of Christmas doesn't bring on their own manger scene, right?"

Surprise showed on Buck's face for a brief second. "There's no plan at this time," he said even more sternly, "to bring on a manger scene." He was beginning to feel that at any moment something was going to happen. Like Farrah Fawcett Scraggs coming up the driveway, deciding not to run away after all. "I haven't got the authority to permit any alternative programs," he told them. "Nancyville is still under a court order not to have any religious Christmas displays of any kind on the courthouse lawn tomorrow night."

"Will you be there?" one of the TV crew called.

Buck peered into the rain, trying to locate the voice. "Yes, I'll be there," he answered.

"Are your deputies armed?" the same voice asked.

"Well yes," Buck said, "they're always armed."

Too late, he saw what was happening. *County sheriff will confront Joseph, Mary, and Baby Jesus at courthouse with armed deputies.* He'd bet anything that was the way it was going to come out on the evening news. He could have kicked himself.

The TV news people were looking excited and happy at this element in their story, but the Hare Krishnas stopped their circling and came to stand at the steps, looking alarmed.

Buck's face felt like granite, but he tried for a smile. "Well, no matter what's planned for tomorrow night," he began, "Nancyville welcomes all—"

"Okay, that's a wrap," the cameraman said to the TV sound man. "Thank you, Sheriff." They turned their backs and abruptly walked off toward their van.

Seeing the TV news crew call it a day, the Hare Krishnas filed toward their vehicle, hopped inside, and pulled shut the doors.

At that moment Kevin Black Badger chose to arrive at the end of the driveway in a county patrol car, lights flashing. Buck leaped from the porch.

"Hey," Black Badger said, sticking a long leg out of the patrol car. He watched interestedly as the Hare Krishnas' van backed to turn out of the drive to the faint hum of *hare ram* chanting. "What goes on, Sheriff? I was told you need me to track a run-away child?"

Buck reached down and dragged his deputy out of the patrol car. The TV crew was still in the drive-way, close enough to hear. "Open your mouth again," Buck growled, "and I'll put you on a month's suspension."

Kevin's eyes widened. "Yes, *sir*," he said.

Buck led him toward the house.

Scarlett met them at the door. She had on her denim jacket, jeans, and a red sweater, and looked beautiful and determined. "What was that all about?" she demanded. "Are those people going to look for Farrie?"

Kevin Black Badger stopped short, transfixed. His black eyes took in Scarlett Scraggses' dark hair flow-ing becomingly over her shoulders, her trim, lus-cious figure, and he reacted with an appreciative quiver.

Buck pushed him out of the doorway. Now rec-ognition dawned in the deputy's eyes. Kevin Black Badger recoiled. "Sheriff, I swear, but isn't she—this —she looks like—"

"Scraggs," Buck said tersely. "She's a Scraggs." He put his hand in the middle of his deputy's back and pushed him down the hall. As he opened the door to the parlor he explained in a few words who Scar-lett was, and how she had come to be his Christmas houseguest. "There are two of them, Devil Anse's granddaughters. They're runaways, and Susan Hud-dleston is in Atlanta taking a long holiday." Buck couldn't keep the bitterness out of his voice. "I've got custody until she returns."

"Well," Kevin said, "that's something." He seemed to shake himself. "Who's the missing child you want me to track?"

Before Buck could answer, Scarlett cried, "It's my little sister, she's run away, and I need to get out there!" Whirling, she made for the door. "I want to go in the patrol car so I can look for her."

Kevin Black Badger rushed forward to open it. "That's a good idea," he said with considerable enthusiasm. "I'll just drive you around, Miss Scr—"

"*Never mind!*" Buck reached over the deputy's shoulder and slammed the door, forcefully. Somehow the idea of Black Badger riding around with Scarlett Scraggs all afternoon in the patrol car did not make him happy. Not with that look on Black Badger's face.

"You're going to track on foot," Buck told him, taking a perverse pleasure in seeing the deputy's face fall. "I want you to do this whole area and the woods in back of the house."

The woods in back of the house covered virtually all of Makim's Mountain. They were thick enough to keep Black Badger busy for a week.

"I've already called in an All Points Bulletin," Buck went on, "so there'll be cars patrolling the immediate vicinity. The missing child's only ten years old or so, let's hope she can't get very far. And," he added, remembering, "she doesn't walk too good."

At his words Scarlett gave a low cry and started for the door again. "You can't keep me here! I've got to get out there and look for her myself!"

Buck caught her and motioned to Black Badger that he could leave.

"You've got to stay here, Scarlett," he said, holding her in spite of her struggles. "When the patrols come back with your sister she's going to be cold and tired and wet. She may even be running a fever." He knew how she worried about her little sister getting sick. "You've got to be here in the house to look after her."

He felt her go slack in his arms. "She's out there, just walking around in the rain," she whimpered. "Farrie's worried because we've got no home, no place to go!"

She was tearing him apart. Buck tightened his arms around her and bent his head to kiss her lightly, on those rosy, tempting lips. More a gesture of comfort, he told himself, than anything else.

But that kiss was fated to be something more. A *lot* more. She seemed to shudder, then opened her mouth to respond to him. It was as though lightning struck them both. A sort of rainbow-hued, dazzling display of earthly delight that sent Buck's head spinning and his knees to shaking. With a groan, he deepened the kiss and drew her closer.

But only for an instant.

With a howl, Scarlett Scraggs wrenched herself so violently away from him that Buck staggered back in stunned surprise. While his head was still reluctantly clearing she yelled: "Don't touch me!"

"What the devil?" Buck exploded. He rubbed the stabbing pain in his bad arm.

"Yes, the devil!" Scarlett Scraggs's beautiful breasts heaved furiously under the denim jacket. *"Devil Anse!*

136

I know what my grandpa's offered you, he *told* me!" Her lip curled, contemptuous. "Did you just make up your mind this minute?"

He'd told her?

Dumbfounded, Buck rubbed the back of his neck. Now it was getting a bit clearer. Blast the old villain! He'd told his own granddaughter he'd offered her as a bribe to the county sheriff! "Scarlett," Buck began, "I—"

"He said if you agreed to it," she spat at him, "I was to act nice to you or he'd come and see that I did!"

Buck stared at her. It had been a bad afternoon, but this finally made him lose his temper.

"Now listen." He pointed his finger at her. "Don't you get it in your head that your vile, low-minded relative can bribe me, even with anything as damned near irresistible as you are. I may lose my head over you, but it won't be because your grandfather thinks he's calling every shot, in or out of bed. No," Buck shouted, "if I'm going to fall in love I'll do it on my own damned time!"

Scarlett stood still for a long moment, her mouth open. *"Fall in love?"*

"Forget it," Buck snarled. He turned away. "Just get what I said out of your head, because nothing's going to happen. I may have made a fool of myself, but I won't do it again."

She followed him toward the parlor, biting her lip. *Fall in love.* That's what he'd said. But not because Devil Anse had anything to do with it.

That meant he'd thought it over and decided not to take up the free trial offer! Scarlett gasped in amazement. It put a whole new light on things, considering the way that she was beginning to feel about him, too.

She didn't know why she was so happy, except now she knew that Buck Grissom wasn't the kind of man her grandpa could twist around his finger! Scarlett regarded him with new eyes as he paced up and down.

"The reason Farrie ran away," she said softly, "was because I told her we couldn't stay here. I told her that Devil Anse was going to make you do something you shouldn't do, and it would mean trouble for all of us. So I guess Farrie couldn't face up to it, having to go away in spite of everything. She's just disappeared."

He wasn't listening. He strode across the room, massaging the back of his neck furiously. "Damn Susan Huddleston! If the kid gets pneumonia I'll have a damned court case on my hands. 'Illegal harboring of a minor.'" He groaned aloud. "Is that a charge? Damned if I know. What else could they sue me for?"

He turned, suddenly distracted by a thought. "I should have told Black Badger to take the damned dog. He says it could be good for tracking. He should have thought of that himself. I'll call him on the Blazer radio—"

He suddenly stopped short. "The *dog!* Where's the infernal dog?"

Scarlett gaped at him. "Demon?"

"It isn't with your little sister, it came in with me! But *where is it?*"

She shook her head. "I don't know."

"You don't know," he repeated, looking around the parlor. "The confounded thing's never more than a foot from me, it never lets me alone. But since we came into the house it's disappeared. That means," Buck said, starting for the door, "it's got to be somewhere in here."

He slammed off toward the kitchen, calling the dog. A few seconds later he came back down the hall. Scarlett heard his steps on the stairs.

She probably should help, she thought. It wasn't like Demon to go missing like that, and was too bad Demon wasn't with Farrie. If Demon was there to look after her little sister it would help a lot. Especially if they didn't find Farrie before it got dark.

With a sudden lump in her throat, Scarlett found she didn't want to think about that. "Demon!" she yelled.

There was no sound from the dining room. Almost no sound at all where she was, in the parlor, except for a faint thumping from behind the big, flashing Christmas tree.

Buck came back. "The dog can't be with her," he was saying to himself, "Farrie was missing before I got home."

He stood in the middle of the room, head cocked, listening. Then he seemed to detect something, for with a quick movement he made a lunge for the other side of the tree. Crouching, Buck dragged a big black animal out from the far corner behind it. "Gotcha," he whooped.

At any other time the thing would have taken his arm off. Now the Scraggs dog lay unresisting, as big as some felled black bear, on its back with its feet and legs hanging limply.

"It's been hiding," Buck told Scarlett. "You've been hiding, you monster, haven't you? Lying back there behind the tree hiding from everybody. But you just gave yourself away wagging that damned tail."

She was puzzled. "Why would Demon do something like that?"

"Because," Buck said, seizing a hind leg and spinning the cowering dog on its back until its head pointed toward him, "it knows something we don't know. It knows where your sister is."

Scarlett sucked in her breath. "Demon *knows?*"

He smiled grimly. "When I remembered Kevin Black Badger saying what a good tracker your dog would make, I knew that if your sister was really missing, the dog would be out in the rain looking for her. We wouldn't be able to keep it in the house. Instead of that, the thing goes to hide behind the Christmas tree."

"Demon," Scarlett said, bending over the dog, "you stop this fooling around and go get Farrie if you know where she is."

"Oh, it knows." Buck reached under the huge dog and tried to roll it onto its feet. He got it halfway, and then Demon fell back, all four legs waving.

"I'll bet I know what happened." Scarlett looked thoughtful. "Wherever Farrie's gone to, I'll bet Farrie told Demon not to let on where it was."

Buck cursed. As well as he could, he dragged the dog to a sitting position. It promptly slid back down again, tail wagging cravenly.

He stood over the Scraggs dog, feeling murderous. "Go get Farrah Fawcett Scraggs," he told it, "or I'll haul you down to the jail and lock you in a cold cell for the night without any food."

At the word "jail" the animal stopped wagging its tail and rolled its eyes up at him. "I think Demon knows what that means," Scarlett said.

It was a Scraggs dog. It would.

"*Two* nights in jail, then," Buck snapped. "Go get Farrah Fawcett. Or do you want to try for three?"

The dog rolled over, groaning, and slowly got to its feet. "Oh, Demon!" Scarlett jumped up, excited. "Good dog! You're gonna go find her!"

Buck couldn't resist giving the dog a shove on its hindquarters with his booted foot. "It's been lying around here hiding," he growled, "when I've got every man I can spare out in this weather looking for her."

"Demon loves Farrie," Scarlett said, following them as the dog started for the hall. "She'll do anything Farrie tells her to. If Farrie told Demon not to let on where she was, then Demon wouldn't do it."

"Are you going up?" They stood at the foot of the steps, which Demon regarded with indifferent interest. "She's upstairs somewhere, isn't she?"

He couldn't believe he was carrying on a conversation with the Scraggses' monstrous beast who, according to Scarlett, kept secrets. Like where the little sister was.

Slowly, tail wagging, the black dog started up the staircase. At the top it turned away from the bedrooms and padded toward the front of the house.

"I know where she's going!" Scarlett darted past

Buck. "Farrie's in your mother's little sewing room, I'll bet you anything she is!"

Buck hurried down the corridor, trying not to get tangled in the dog. They went up the stairs and at the door to the tower room Demon flopped down heavily and buried its head between its paws. Scarlett tried the doorknob.

"The sewing room's locked," Buck told her.

"Farrie can pick locks, she's real good at it." She rattled the door handle. "She could get in there if she wanted to."

"Why in hell would she want to do that?" Buck stepped over the dog and bent and put his eye to the keyhole. He couldn't see anything, it was dark. "Farrie?" he called, experimentally.

There was no answer.

He turned to Scarlett. Her face was white. She held one fist to her mouth, trying not to cry out. "It's dark in there," she moaned. "Farrie went in there in the dark to hide."

There was no heat in there, Buck knew, but he didn't say it. He felt a slow coil of fear unwind in his belly. Why would a child go hide in a dark room as cold as this one, unless she didn't expect to come out? Buck braced himself for something unpleasant. "Stand back," he told Scarlett.

Scarlett drew a deep breath. "You going to shoot the lock off?"

"You've been watching too much television. No, I'm going to use a key."

He took out his key ring, found the right one, and unlocked the door. There was no sound from inside while he was doing this, and no sound when he swung it open.

The outside shutters were drawn and it was so dark Buck stumbled over some boxes groping for the light switch.

Scarlett charged past him. "Oh, Farrie, Farrie, my poor baby," she screamed.

The light didn't come on, the bulb was burned out. Buck couldn't see what Scarlett was doing, but he heard her sobs. "Move aside," he told her, as he pushed the dog out of the way and swung his legs over a trunk and came down on the other side. He saw the old football jacket. That was all there seemed to be, the jacket, and a pair of scrawny legs, but he recognized the lime-colored tights and the stained high-top sneakers. Buck bent and slid both hands under the bundle that was the youngest Scraggs.

When he picked her up her head fell back and he saw the pale, wizened face, seemingly lifeless, the eyes closed tight.

A little too tight, Buck noted. In his experience, when someone was unconscious the eyelids came loosely together, relaxed. Miss Farrah Fawcett Scraggs was playing possum.

But that was not to say she wasn't a pathetic little possum. In his arms, Buck found as he started for the door, she was as weightless as ever and even her clothes were cold to the touch. Up there in the dark tower room it must have felt like the tomb itself.

Poor little pixie, he thought, she'd probably got more than she'd bargained for. She was rigid with cold.

Still, he reminded himself, she could have come out at any time.

"Farrie," Scarlett moaned, following them down the stairs and out into the hall. "Why did she go and do it? She near froze in there!"

Buck maneuvered around her, kicking the dog out of the way. "The bedroom," he told her. "I'm going to put her in your bed. You go downstairs and fix her something hot to drink." As Scarlett wavered, he snapped, "Go ahead, my mother's got some cocoa mix somewhere."

Scarlett ran down the stairs. Buck carried Farrie into his sister's bedroom. When he leaned over her to put her on the bed, she opened her eyes. He hung over her, finding he couldn't get her little hands unlocked from around his neck.

"You'll be okay," Buck said, trying to pry her fingers apart. "You can let go of me now."

The sad little eyes looked up at him.

"Don't make no use," the child whispered. "If I let you go, we still can't stay noplace. There's no place at all for Scarlett and me."

There was no need to deny it, she spoke the truth. There was no place for Scraggs children and other outcasts; day in and day out in the southern mountains he saw it, and his deputies did, too. Farrie wasn't the only one.

"We'll work on it," Buck told her. "You just relax."

He knew that wasn't good enough to tell a wisp of a child who had wanted to crawl into a cold dark place and disappear, but it was the best he could do at the moment.

"Just lie back and shut your eyes for now," Buck said. "And tomorrow you can show me how you get into locked rooms."

Eyes closed, Farrie smiled.

Fourteen

SCARLETT LAY BESIDE FARRIE IN THE BIG tester bed, listening to the wind roar around the corners of the Grissoms' house. The rain had stopped. Through the ruffled curtains dark clouds scudded before a full moon. The wind and weather had changed; it would be much colder in the morning.

It was cold *now*, Scarlett thought with a small, comfortable shiver. In the night, in the dark, the deep, soft bed was a wonderful place, a warm nest with fancy ruffles of the canopy covering them overhead, where she could still hear the comforting sound of the furnace cutting on and off.

She reached out and gently rolled Farrie's curled, bony little body up against her. When she held her fingers against her sister's cheek she found her still cool to the touch. It was nothing short of a miracle that she hadn't run a fever—Farrie, who could run a fever over practically nothing when she wasn't happy. But her little sister had bounced back from her adventure, if you could call it that, and had even eaten a good dinner from the tray Buck had brought to her room.

They'd argued over whether Farrie should have had hot soup, even after the hot chocolate, but Scarlett didn't have time to make soup. And Farrie had gobbled up what she'd fixed, anyway: a whole baked stuffed potato with bacon and creamed spinach, then the grilled tomatoes with cheese, the green peas, garbanzo beans, candied yams, and even half a box of Oreo cookies she'd found in the pantry.

"My God," Buck had said, watching her. "How can she eat like that and still stay that size?"

Scarlett said thoughtfully, "I think she's gaining weight."

"And growing, too." Farrie looked up at them with her bright eyes. "I think I growed some, too, while I was here."

Buck had groaned.

Nevertheless, Scarlett thought, watching the cold moonlight dance across the ceiling, he had told her he wasn't going to give in to Devil Anse and take a bribe, even if the bribe was Scarlett. He'd even called Devil Anse "vile," and "low-minded." Scarlett supposed you could call her grandpa that; she'd heard all her life there wasn't anything a lowdown Scraggs wouldn't do. And Devil Anse sure set the example.

Sheriff Buck Grissom was a brave man, Scarlett thought, and he had a kind heart. He'd fed Farrie hot chocolate from a spoon, taken her pulse, then sat on the bed beside her while Farrie ate and talked to him about opening locks.

"You know that Master lock number three?" Farrie loved being important; she hiked up in the bed next to Buck so she could look right in his face. "Like the one that you got in your gun case downstairs in the den with the twelve-gauge shotguns, and the automatic weapons like the AK-47? Well, they say in those ads in gun magazines that they can't be picked. But they *can!*"

He'd looked skeptical. "That lock has a guarantee. That's why it's on my gun case. Those are confiscated illegal weapons."

"I know that. But what you do is"—Farrie gestured in the air with her thin little fingers—"you get you two pieces of wire like from a coat hanger. The first piece you bend into a L-shape and slide right in at the opening where you put the teeth of the key, and you hold down the ratchet with it."

Buck raised his eyebrows.

She nodded knowingly. "Then while you're holding down the ratchet," Farrie went on, "you slide the second piece of wire to push the tumblers out of the way. Then you rotate the first piece of wire with that L-shape and it will go click! Nice and easy. You got your number three Master lock open."

"You've got to be kidding." Buck stared at her. "Did some of your—ah, somebody teach you how to do all of this?"

"My uncle Lyndon Baines," Farrie said proudly. "Only I'm better than he is, now."

Scarlett had come up in a hurry to take what was left of the dinner away and tell Farrie to slide down in the bed and close her eyes. It was time to end that conversation right where it was.

"We don't say no prayers," she'd explained as she tucked Farrie in. "I've heard a lot of people always say their prayers at bedtime, but my great-aunt Lutie Scraggs used to say: 'Don't cry and you won't be sorry. And don't pray for nothing. That way you're not disappointed.' "

He gave her an odd look. "That's quite a philosophy."

She shrugged. "I don't know what you call it, but it's what Scraggses do."

Farrie told Buck she wanted him to kiss her goodnight. He had leaned down to let her wind her arms around him and give him a big smack on the cheek.

So it looked like Sheriff Buck didn't hold a grudge, Scarlett thought as she watched them. And his deputies didn't seem to mind, except the big Indian deputy, Kevin Black Badger, who had come in pretty mad after a long time in the cold on the mountain because nobody had thought to tell him.

Now, lying in bed, Scarlett could let herself sigh with relief at how well everything had turned out. Farrie was safe, and nobody seemed to blame her for acting the way she did.

If there was any trouble, she thought with a small frown, it had to do with the television newscast, and the people with cars and trucks in the driveway earlier.

Buck had said he was going to be in the den to see the newscast. Scarlett had been in the kitchen getting supper warmed up. What made her notice it at all was that she heard Buck cussing. Curious, she'd come to the door to see what was going on.

There on the television screen was the figure of Sheriff Buck Grissom saying there couldn't be any living manger scene at the courthouse because of a court order.

Then, while Scarlett was still admiring how nice Buck looked, big and handsome in his uniform, the camera moved up close on his face as he said that he had armed deputies, if necessary, to keep any manger scene away.

You could tell right away that what Buck had said about armed deputies wasn't right. You could see it right there on his face that he knew it, too, before the camera swung away and the man in the television news studio came back on.

A moment later the telephone had started ringing. Instead of eating his dinner that Scarlett had fixed, Buck had answered one call after another until he finally gave up and went upstairs to see how Farrie was getting along. He came down again later to check the news, and Scarlett went to clean up the kitchen. When the news came on again, the telephone started to ring. It hadn't stopped ringing, even late as it was.

Scarlett went out on the upstairs landing where she could see the light from the den and hear the rumble of Buck's voice, still answering calls. Whoever they were, people in Nancyville, they ought to leave him alone, she thought. Deputies *were* armed. He was only telling the truth.

She couldn't help remembering how he had looked as he sat on the edge of the bed feeding

Farrie hot chocolate from a cup. Or the look on his face as he'd carried her out of the tower room. Or when he'd searched for her pulse. You wouldn't think those big hands could find a spot on a little girl's skinny wrist to take her pulse, but they had.

It was just too bad that some people hadn't liked what they saw on TV, because their sheriff was a brave man. A good man. She had never met a man like him before.

I'm in love with him, Scarlett thought, surprised.

It was such a strange, totally unexpected feeling that she sat straight up in bed, staring at the spot of moonlight falling on the carpet by the window.

Was she sure? She didn't want to make a big mistake again like she had the other night, coming to his room. But Sheriff Buck Grissom made her heart stop just watching him. And the feeling that she just couldn't wait for him to kiss her hung around her like a homeless cat practically all the time.

It was love, all right, because it felt just like she'd heard other people say—sort of warm and excited and feeling happy whenever she thought about Buck. It was, Scarlett realized, probably the most wonderful thing that had ever happened to her. That's why she hadn't recognized it right away; she just wasn't used to having wonderful things happen.

But now, how everything had changed! For one thing, she didn't have to force herself to do anything, she didn't have to please Farrie and trick him into marriage. And she didn't have to please Devil Anse, who wanted to bribe Buck and make him do something crooked.

No, she thought, almost hugging herself, she was

in *love* with Sheriff Buck Grissom. She could please *herself!*

It made her so happy she couldn't wait to tell him. She slipped her bare feet over the edge of the bed and started for the door.

The darkened house smelled like Christmas, filled with the fragrance of the spruce tree in the parlor. The prisms in the hall's ceiling fixture winked sparks of light as Scarlett hurried under them.

What should she say? Just tell Buck that she'd just found out she was in love with him?

Scarlett hesitated at the door to the den, hearing his voice on the telephone. He was talking, not to someone about what had happened on the television news, she realized, but to his mother. It was Mrs. Grissom's nightly call from Chicago. She always called after eleven because they had a different time in Chicago, Buck had explained.

Scarlett stood by the half-open door to the den, not knowing now whether she wanted to go in. She hadn't known about places in America having different times. "Zones," Buck had called them. But then she was pretty ignorant; she'd never finished her last year of high school because Devil Anse had made her drop out.

If a person was in love with someone like Buck Grissom, Scarlett thought, they would have to give some thought to something like that. Her grandpa, Ancil Scraggs, and all the things he'd done. And how much school she had missed.

She'd already seen the woman they said Buck had once been engaged to: Susan Huddleston, the county social worker. You could see Susan Huddleston was pretty much what a sheriff would look for in a wife. Not, she told herself, slowly taking a step back from the doorway, some wild Scraggs from Catfish Holler.

The happy feeling faded away. Scarlett knew now that she didn't want Buck to feel that he was being forced into anything. Hadn't he already told her he didn't intend to make a fool of himself?

She bit her lip. She supposed he could do that, make a fool of himself with Scarlett Scraggs, old Devil Anse Scraggs's granddaughter. Especially if she came down after eleven o'clock at night in her bare feet and only a secondhand church nightgown and tried to tell him that she had some crazy idea that she loved him.

The happy feeling was gone now, replaced with a sad, hollow place in her middle.

There couldn't be anything much better than to live in this house, and make a home for Farrie, and be Buck Grissom's wife. But look at her! She didn't even have bedroom slippers to put on her feet. When she got dressed in the morning she put on somebody else's clothes. And she didn't have a home. Neither did her little sister.

It had been all right to pretend that she could trick Buck Grissom into marrying her. Or even to know that Devil Anse had tried to use her to bribe him. But it was a different thing entirely when you'd just found out you were in love.

And that maybe he wouldn't care.

Shoulders drooping, Scarlett turned and padded back to the stairs.

* * *

Buck was glad to know from his mother's call that his sister and the kids were fine, and that her husband was diagnosed, now, with a concussion and not the skull fracture they'd all feared. As soon as he hung up, though, the telephone rang again.

Buck snatched it up. He was dog-tired and wanted to go to bed but it seemed like half the town of Nancyville had to talk to him. It had been that way since six o'clock. This time his caller was the mayor. "Yeah, Harry," Buck said wearily.

"Buck, listen," the mayor said. The evening's constant talking had reduced his voice to a rasp. "As you know, most of the city council are still here at my house, with the exception of Steve Morrisey and Britta Jergensen—Britta had to go home and let her babysitter go. But we've been looking over some of the counteractive measures that have been suggested, and we've decided to—ah, commit to a few."

"We don't need any of that, Harry," Buck said. "In spite of what you think you heard on television, the sheriff's department of Jackson County is not going to be down at the courthouse tomorrow night with a cadre of deputies to use force on any living manger scene. Because there isn't going to *be* any manger scene."

"Now, you don't know that, Buck," the mayor said quickly. "There were a lot of people looking at Channel Ten tonight, and they heard what you said."

"That was just something dreamed up by those Atlanta news people," Buck maintained. "Nobody had said anything about a manger scene or using deputies until the TV people showed up. Harry, that team would have been happy as hell if they'd gotten me to say that I was going to run Joseph and Mary and the kid that won the Best Baby Jesus contest off the courthouse lawn at gunpoint!"

"That's just the problem," the mayor said hoarsely. "Junior Whitford came over here a little while ago with most of his Committee for the Real Meaning of Christmas, and they'd been watching Channel Ten, too. I'll say it to you, Buck, although I won't say it to them—that damned committee's got their heads turned by all the publicity. They've decided they're going to have a manger scene after all!"

Buck surveyed the wall before him bleakly. "They can't. There's a court order."

"Court order, fiddle-faddle!" the mayor burst out. "They think they're going to storm the courthouse! They've already called Channel Ten, Junior tells me, to tell them what they're going to do."

And Channel Ten loved it, Buck thought.

"We had to put on our thinking caps," the mayor went on. "There we were, except for Britta and Steve Morrisey, trying to come up with a new approach."

Buck said cautiously, "You're not thinking of those damned fireworks, are you?"

The council had learned that in a pinch they could use the leftover supplies of fireworks from the last municipal Fourth of July celebration, which was not as strange as it sounded: fireworks were a part of southern Christmases, even though the custom was dying out somewhat.

"Well, I think we ought to go with the fireworks," the mayor was saying, "although I know you don't like them, Buck. But the idea is to provide so much entertainment tomorrow night that—uh, people won't look kindly on any interruptions from Junior and folks I won't mention. We've just had an offer from Ronnie Dance, who runs an outfit that specializes in dropping Santa Clauses during the holiday season."

"Dropping Santa Clauses?" Buck straightened up, surprised in spite of himself. "What the hell's that?"

"The big operators bring their Santa Clauses in by helicopter, Buck," the voice on the telephone explained a little apologetically. "You know, Santa just steps right out of the chopper in the parking lot and into the nearest J.C. Penney's or what have you. Ronnie doesn't have a helicopter, he runs a sky-diving service in the summertime out of a Cessna 206. Santa Claus-dropping is just his off-season business. But he can drop a skydiver in a Santa uniform onto a circle that's been already drawn on the asphalt at the shopping mall. Most of Ronnie's Santas used to be paratroopers; they kind of look for that target."

"Harry," Buck said, keeping his voice even with an effort, "we don't need a skydiving Santa at the Living Christmas Tree tomorrow night. There's going to be enough going on."

"Buck, I can't refuse it!" the mayor rasped. "Ronnie's offered it free, after Santa does his jump up at the K Mart in Toccoa. It's a good thing the Living Christmas Tree's at sundown. Ronnie says he can just squeeze Santa in as the last jump of the day, and it won't cost us a dime."

"Harry," Buck said, his temper beginning to slip, "you and the city council just consider that I'm responsible for maintaining law and order in this county, and I don't know about being able to do that if you're going to encourage anybody to stage their own demonstrations tomorrow night—"

"Nobody encouraged Junior and that damned committee," the mayor shouted, "that was his own idea!"

"—and pile a fireworks display and a Santa jump from a Cessna on top of it, while the people who worked hard on all this are trying to give the Living Christmas Tree their concert."

The mayor made choking noises, trying to interrupt, but Buck went on. "Harry, it's going to be pure hell if the council does even half this stuff, and then you want to throw the whole enchilada right in my lap! Now, you just tell those people you got in your house thinking up these bright ideas to go home and get some sleep."

"Dammit, I'm not going to do that!" the mayor fired back. "Those people, as you call them, know there's a need to show we got some civilizing influence up here, and that we're not a bunch of jerks and hillbillies like they tried to show tonight on TV. As for you, Sheriff Grissom," he said sarcastically, "*you're* the one what shot off your mouth about armed deputies that are going to see to it we don't have any unofficial manger scenes!"

"Now just a damned minute," Buck said.

But the mayor had hung up.

Buck put the telephone back in its cradle with a groan of pent-up exasperation. The city council and the mayor had panicked, egged on by all those Nancyville citizens who had kept the telephone lines hot that night. The town had gotten upset enough about the original injunction over not having the living manger scene downtown. Now he knew his remark on TV, which seemed to say he would have deputies holding off any illegal Mary and Infant Jesus at the courthouse, had struck a nerve.

Damn, Buck thought, massaging the back of his neck furiously, he was beginning to hate Christmas!

He turned off the television in the den. The Scraggs dog got out from behind the couch and followed him as he went down the hall to the parlor to put out the lights on the Christmas tree. "I see you're with me once more," he told it.

The dog trotted along beside him, wagging its tail.

Buck stood gazing at the huge winking, glittering spruce for a long moment, suddenly realizing that since the Scraggs sisters were going to be with him for Christmas, somebody had to buy them presents.

What could you buy for the lock-picking little sister? he wondered. The contents of the Nancyville Hardware Store's security department, so she could practice? A Rubik's cube?

That didn't sound like such a bad idea. Buck bent to finger a crayoned, cotton-bearded paper Santa Claus he remembered from the second grade.

And clothes. Farrie seemed to like clothes, the

stranger the better. At least he could get both of them more than one pair of shoes.

And Scarlett?

Ah, *Scarlett*, Buck thought, still fingering the forgotten paper Santa Claus in his hand. What would he like to buy for her?

She wasn't like Susan, he thought, bemused. She was a different person in her own right, soft and sparkling behind that tough Scraggs façade and, when you came down to it, an enchanting mystery. Both she and her sister were fascinated with the old Grissom house and what it represented, the kind of home they'd never had. The littlest one couldn't keep her hands off the Christmas tree. And Scarlett was a natural-born chef.

Something for cooking, Buck thought, maybe one of those hand mixers. A set of chef's knives. A frilly apron.

Black silk underwear, he thought suddenly. The idea of Scarlett in a frilly apron with nothing but black bikini panties and a black lace bra on under it made Buck's fingers contract convulsively.

Looking down, he saw what he had done. He mashed the paper Santa Claus back into shape and flicked away the loosened parts of its beard.

You had to have a taste for trouble, he told himself as he turned out the Christmas tree lights, shoved the dog out of the way, and went out into the downstairs hall, to even think about Scarlett O'Hara Scraggs. Any professional lawman who gave a passing thought to the granddaughter of one of the state's biggest criminals was out of his damned mind.

At the top of the stairs, he paused at their bedroom door and listened. Asleep, both of them.

Buck felt oddly disappointed. He'd almost wanted to find Scarlett awake, so he could talk to her. Maybe she had some ideas about this infernal mess with the council's skydiving Santa Claus and fireworks. She seemed to have a pretty sharp mind.

He stood there, shifting from one foot to the other, not wanting to do anything as boring as go to bed, even though he was dog-tired.

At that moment the door opened.

The hall was dark and there was no light in his sister's bedroom, but he knew at once it was Scarlett.

"What?" she said in a husky, sleepy voice.

Buck could just make out that cloud of dark hair, the pale oval of her face, the shadowy pools of her eyes. She was wearing the Atlanta Braves nightshirt that clung to her beautiful breasts and came only to the middle of her long legs. Buck tried not to look at it.

"I see you're up after all," he said, promptly cursing himself for the year's stupidest observation.

"I heard you come up the stairs," she murmured.

Buck knew he should say good night and turn to go to his room, but he didn't. Instead, he stood drinking in the sight of Scarlett Scraggs, her lissom form in the nightshirt, her lovely face, her curving mouth that was sweetly, seductively, parted.

As if to ask, Buck thought suddenly, the question he'd never answered that night in his room. *Aren't you going to kiss me again?*

"Scarlett," Buck said hoarsely. Those luminous

eyes regarded him cautiously. "Are you—ah, comfortable in—in there?"

She considered that. "Well, it's nice. Farrie especially likes the bed."

Bed, Buck thought. It would have to be that word. He resolutely put thoughts of aprons and black lingerie out of his mind. Instead, he studied her hand resting against the doorjamb: the long, graceful fingers, the delicate wrist, amazed all over again that something so beautiful, so exquisitely fashioned, could be produced by that cesspool of criminal genes, the Scraggses. *She hasn't had a chance*, Buck told himself.

He cleared his throat. "Don't need a window open, or anything?"

"No." That sad, slightly quizzical look was still there.

She's wondering what I'm doing, standing here, Buck thought desperately. *What I want from her.*

He felt a slight sheen of sweat break out on the back of his neck, under his collar. They were so close now they were almost touching. With a little effort he could put his good arm around her, hold her warm, slender body in the Atlanta Braves nightshirt up against him, as he had before.

He couldn't leave, yet he sensed something was different. If she was unhappy about something he wanted to comfort her. With a groan, Buck reached out with his left arm and scooped Scarlett Scraggs to him. He heard her gasp before he covered her mouth with his own.

Kissing Scarlett Scraggs was dangerous; it got

better each time. She flowed into his arms, soft and tantalizing, sweetly giving—Buck drowned in that kiss. He could barely tear himself away.

When he looked down into Scarlett's face, he saw her eyes were still closed. "Oh," she was murmuring softly. "Oh!"

The astonishing part of this whole thing was not that kissing Scarlett O'Hara Scraggs was a sweet seventh wonder of the world, a dazzling trip through outer space and back again, but that they didn't need to talk, say anything at all. The kiss said it all for them, a tender, fragile bubble of feeling that was wonderful.

Buck, still locked in the magic, didn't want to let her go. It was Scarlett who pulled away. "I gotta go," she said.

He supposed she was right. But he couldn't help thinking she didn't seem very enthusiastic about what had just happened. Not the way she'd been before.

Buck thought he'd detected an odd sadness. There was certainly no mistaking the faint, teary wobble in her voice.

"Scarlett, wait," Buck said.

But the door closed softly. He stared at it, still not able to figure out what this was all about. She'd acted like he'd broken her heart instead of kissing her.

He was damned if it made any sense, he thought grumpily as he opened the door to his bedroom and the Scraggs dog rushed past him to leap on his bed. But that's what you got being involved with the

Scraggs tribe. What was it Susan had said? *They were hardly rewarding.*

But for a moment, Buck knew, he'd held a soft armful of heaven in his arms. It was a long time before he got to sleep.

Fifteen

"THIS IS THE LAST REHEARSAL," MR. RA-venwood shouted. When the talking and giggling in the upper levels of the Living Christmas Tree platform didn't die down, he took a deep breath and yelled into the bullhorn, "If I could have your attention—ATTENTION—please?"

"It's COLD," someone yelled back.

It was. The cold front that had come through in the night had written fern frost on the window glass of parked automobiles, frozen the ground, and rendered human beings blue with cold after more than fifteen minutes. The upper levels of the wooden tree were chilled to the bone, having been there since seven A.M. From time to time some of the singers breathed into their hands and looked up at the sky, hoping for a little heat, but the sun hung obstinately behind a bank of gray clouds, and the weather report said it was going to be even colder for the performance that night.

"I wouldn't mind the cold so much," Judy Heamstead whispered to Scarlett, "if I could just move around. My feet are turning numb!"

Scarlett merely nodded. She was busy watching Farrie being hoisted to a spot above them at the top of the tree. Mr. Heamstead and the Presbyterians had worked late the night before, hammering the foothold in place. Her little sister was like an excited little bird perched up there in her blue ski jacket and pompom cap. All of Farrie's dreams were coming true, but Scarlett was having a hard time fighting down her own misery.

"What's the matter?" Judy Heamstead asked, leaning to her. "Are you sorry you ran away? Do you miss home?"

Miss Devil Anse and Catfish Holler? Scarlett could only shake her head.

Judy and Scarlett were in full costume for the dress rehearsal, wearing long white gowns over their coats, tinsel halos, and carrying flashlights with big aluminum-foil collars cut to look like stars. The Angels' long skirts made it hard to climb the catwalks, but they were a lot more comfortable than the Bells, who wore red turtleneck sweaters and had stiff cardboard cutouts shaped like red Christmas bells around their faces. Instead of flashlights they carried dinner bells from the Nancyville hardware store, donated by the Downtown Merchants Association.

Scarlett could answer Judy's question by telling her that she hadn't been happy since last night, when she'd realized she was in love with Buck Grissom. But Judy would probably laugh at something as stupid as that.

Above them men were lifting Farrie into place.

"You think you can sing up there?" one of them teased. Scarlett heard Farrie laugh.

"There *is* something wrong," Judy insisted, peering at her. "Are you all right at the Grissoms' house? Sheriff Grissom been mean to you, has he?"

"Mean to me? Oh, *no!*" Scarlett swallowed. "He's been real nice. Buck's—really kind."

"Buck?" Judy's eyes widened. *"Buck?* Oh Scarlett, is that why you're looking so miserable? Are you stuck on handsome ole *Buck Grissom?"*

Scarlett couldn't look at Judy. "What are we going to sing?" She juggled her flashlight to open the music. "Are we on the last number?"

Judy was staring at Scarlett fixedly. "They say Buck hasn't dated anybody since he broke up with Susan Huddleston. Oh, tell me, did Buck Grissom come on to you? Did he kiss you? What was it like?"

Scarlett's face was burning with humiliation. If people in Nancyville thought there was anything going on between her and the sheriff, they'd think the worst.

She started to say something, but just at that moment the band teacher raised his arms, brought them down for the beat, and the tree began to sing. Scarlett didn't have her place. She looked across the courthouse lawn and saw early traffic moving around the square. Some cars had already pulled into parking spaces. A fancy blue Dodge pickup truck had just stopped. Two figures got out, an old man with a prophet's white beard, and a younger one.

She saw them look up at the tree. Reese Potter

pointed, calling Devil Anse's attention to Farrie. But the old man's eyes had found Scarlett.

What those eyes silently said froze her to the bones. Her fingers gripped the music pages as Devil Anse's glare, full of an unknown warning, seemed to bore into her skull.

A moment later she saw him take Reese Potter's arm, and they got back in the truck. After a minute, the Dodge pulled out of its space and drove away.

"You don't have to come in the back way," Sheriff Buck Grissom's secretary said, "they're already here."

"So I see." Buck shoved the Scraggs dog out of his way and started toward his office. Unfortunately, the Committee for the Real Meaning of Christmas, with Junior Whitford in front, moved to block his way.

"Sheriff, we hope we're not going to have any trouble with you tonight," Whitford said belligerently. "We come down here this morning to tell you that under the Constitution of the United States we're entitled to our free speech. Ain't that right?" he said, turning to the three men and two women behind him.

They nodded vigorously.

Buck stood with his hands in his Sam Browne belt. The leader of the Committee for the Real Meaning of Christmas was a small, paunchy, middle-aged electrician of undoubtedly sincere convictions. But the last time Buck had heard of Junior he'd been a member of a snake-handling church that his deputies tried to keep their eye on over in Folsom Ridge.

"I'm going to give *you* trouble?" Buck said. "I'm not trying to break the law, Mr. Whitford, you are. We have a court order that says there are to be no displays of religious significance on the courthouse lawn. And it's my job as sheriff of Jackson County to enforce that order."

"With armed deputies?" Junior shrilled. "That's what you said on the television news last night, wasn't it—*armed deputies?*"

"Sheriff," one of the ladies behind Whitford called. She held up her arm, waving several sheets of paper. "We have a petition—"

"Wait!" This was Madelyne Smith, coming to Buck's rescue. She jumped up from her desk and hurried to hand him a pink telephone-message slip. "Sheriff," she said loudly, "I have Mr. Byron Turnipseed on the line from the Georgia State criminal investigation department. Folks"—She turned to the committee, smiling brightly—"I can make an appointment for all of you to meet with Sheriff Grissom if you'll just tell me when you want to see him."

Buck took advantage of Madelyne's strategy to hurry past Junior and his crowd, stumble over the Scraggs beast, enter his office and shut the door.

He sat down behind his desk, feeling winded. He'd never expected to find the committee lying in wait for him when he got to work. It sure wasn't a great way to start his day.

When he looked at Madelyne's pink telephone slip in his hand it said: "Byron Turnipseed is not on the line, Buck, but he did call last night after you left. Mose took the message. The Georgia criminal investigation department wants you to contact them ASAP."

Buck had just lifted the telephone to do that very thing when Deputy Rory Haines entered his office wearing an expression of disgust and pain.

"What's the matter?" Buck said, putting the telephone back down.

Haines lifted a small, naked body by the legs and held it out to him. "You won't believe this, Sheriff, but I found out where them turkeys have gone to."

"I believe it," Buck said, staring at the inert form that the deputy now laid carefully on his desk. "Just tell me."

"A deputy from Union County came down last night with one of these, wanted to know if it was what we had a bulletin out on. Seems half of a little town up there called Deer Run's been just saturated with turkeys. Somebody's selling them out of the back of a truck at about five dollars apiece."

Buck got up, swearing under his breath. "Damn, I haven't been here five minutes. I'm never going to get a chance to do my paperwork." In front of his desk the Scraggs dog was sitting on its haunches, staring at the plump body on his blotter. "Better take back that turkey," he reminded the deputy.

"It's the Piedmont Poultry hijacked truck, ain't it?" Haines said, picking it up.

"Sounds like it. I guess I'll have to go up to Union County and see what they've got."

The deputy followed him to the door, bird in hand. "Sheriff, if you're going up that way, Kevin Black Badger's down with bronchial pneumonia, and wants somebody to bring him his camping stuff he left on his desk. He doesn't want it lying around the office while he's out sick."

Buck nodded.

Moses Holt met them in the outer office with what appeared to be Kevin's things: a stack of blankets and a sheepskin hide, a Coleman stove perched on top, and a sleeping bag. As they went out to the parking lot Buck looked around warily, but Junior and his committee seemed to have left.

"I'll be back around noon," Buck told his deputies as they loaded Black Badger's camping gear in the back of the Blazer. "I have to check out the Living Christmas Tree early and see we've got all our security in place."

The deputies looked at each other.

"Sheriff," Moses Holt said, "there's no possibility we're going to have to fire on anybody, is there? Junior Whitford's a cousin of my wife's sister's brother-in-law and he says—"

"The story all over town is," Haines interrupted, "that the committee is going to try tonight to put a manger scene in place. A sort of Christmas sit-in."

"Yeah, I heard that," Buck said, shoving the dog out of his seat and getting in behind the wheel. "Look, I don't care what kind of rumors they're spreading, if there's a manger sit-in, we'll deal with it the way my dad did in the seventies with the Vietnam War protesters. We will gently remove them from the area in dispute."

As he said it, Buck hoped that if the manger sit-in materialized, the parties involved would come peaceably. And that Jackson County deputies wouldn't have to bodily carry out Joseph, Mary, and some local kid voted Best Baby Jesus. That would make a TV news item Jackson County would never forget.

Both deputies stepped back as he gunned the engine and pulled the Blazer out of the parking lot.

Kevin Black Badger lived out on Route 19, the highway that ran north to Union County and then into North Carolina. Buck was sorry to hear about Kevin's bronchial pneumonia, but told himself it was not all that serious or Kevin would be in the hospital. On the other hand, he wasn't at all sorry that he'd assigned Kevin to search Makim's Mountain instead of driving the patrol car around all afternoon with Scarlett Scraggs.

The sky was overcast and because of the cold there wasn't much traffic. Buck was looking for connecting State Road 165 that would take him into 19 when he came around a curve, doing about sixty, and suddenly saw an old stake-sided truck broken down in the middle of the road.

Buck swerved the Blazer. He had put his sling back on his right arm that morning, and the moment he yanked at the steering wheel he knew that had been a mistake. The Blazer hardly responded to one hand. As he struggled with it a weedy figure in a satin windbreaker and cowboy hat stepped out from behind the broken-down stakebody at the last minute, waving his arms.

The Blazer missed the idiot dancing in front of it, roared off onto the shoulder of the road, then plunged into a stand of shortleaf pines.

It took a moment for Buck to pry himself upright.

The passenger's side door hung open and the Scraggs dog was gone. He'd banged his head, but he wasn't so groggy that he didn't recognize the two faces that appeared at the Blazer's window.

"Well, boy,", Devil Anse said, "we been trackin' you all week and we gotcha. This here's Reese Potter, my granddaughter Scarlett's betrothed, you might say. We're both a mite anxious to ask you a few things. Like when you're gonna make up yore mind."

Scarlett had locked all the doors and windows to the Grissoms' house, but she still kept looking over her shoulder and listening for the sound of trucks or cars in the driveway that might be Devil Anse and the Potters coming for her. Thinking about it, she accidentally stabbed Farrie with the pin she was using to fasten her mistletoe headdress.

"Ow!" Her sister's scream was genuine. "What's the matter with you, Scarlett? You been acting mean as a three-legged cat all day long, but I ain't done nothing to you!"

"No, you haven't," she admitted. She was afraid to tell Farrie of her feeling that something terrible was going to happen. They should have left Nancyville a long time ago. Now Buck Grissom was in trouble with Devil Anse because he hadn't let him bribe him, Reese Potter was hanging around again when she'd thought there'd been an end to all that, and, finally, she was in love with Buck and it was plain he didn't love *her*.

No, last but not least, Scarlett thought, studying her sister standing in front of her in Mr. Ravenwood's Spirit of the Mistletoe costume, there was Farrie. She didn't know how she was going to get Farrie out of Nancyville when her little sister thought all these things that were happening were wonderful. The new life they'd been looking for.

But after Christmas, Scarlett knew, they would be plain old Scraggses again. The social worker, Miss Huddleston, would be back in town and Farrie most likely would be turned over to the court. She had heard enough about the Jackson County welfare department to guess it wasn't likely they'd give Farrie back to their grandpa to raise. They'd put Farrie in a foster home, or a home for children who needed special care—

And Scarlett would never see her again.

"What's the matter, Scarlett?" Farrie peered up into her face. "You look so sad. Aren't you happy we're going to have a Christmas this once?"

Scarlett frowned. "We had Christmas before," she said, jerking the pieces of plastic mistletoe into place. "I got a doll from the church over at Toccoa when I was little, and we had some kind of Christmas nearly every year since you were born. Maybe not so as you'd notice it much, but we had it." She picked up a plastic mistletoe berry that had fallen out of Farrie's headdress and tossed it on the table. "This stuff! Last Christmas I shot real mistletoe out of oak trees and we sold it."

"With Uncle Lyndon Baines's twenty-two," Farrie reminded her.

Scarlett shrugged. "Anybody can shoot mistletoe out of a tree with a shotgun."

"We made fifty-seven dollars," Farrie remembered, "but Grandpa took it away from us."

"Well,"—Scarlett leaned back on her heels to look at Farrie full-length—"that's why we ran away."

Something was happening to her little sister. In her long white angel dress, topped now by the big, full wreath of plastic mistletoe resting on her wiry hair, Farrie glowed. For the first time it seemed to Scarlett that Farrie was looking more like other little girls. Her face wasn't so pinched, she didn't seem so thin, her funny little grin wasn't so elvish. And tonight was Farrie's night.

Mr. Ravenwood had put Farrie on the top of the tree as the Spirit of Mistletoe for the final number. The closing song sung by the entire tree, plus Farrie's solo, would be spectacularly joined by all the church bells in downtown Nancyville: the First Methodist, the Nancyville First Baptist, the Makim's Mountain Presbyterian, and St. George's Episcopal Church, which had a real carillon played by computer program.

"I guess I'm happy we're having Christmas here," Scarlett said reluctantly. There was no need to let her little sister suffer just because she was out of sorts. "It could be a lot worse."

She looked up at the kitchen clock. It was almost noon and she had to fix lunch. That at least would make her feel better, planning something for Farrie and herself to eat from the cookbooks.

Nevertheless, the doleful feeling wouldn't go away. Scarlett wished it was five o'clock, and time for the Heamsteads to pick them up for the performance. But that was still hours away.

* * *

A trickle of blood from the cut on his eyebrow where the cretin in the cowboy hat had hit him made its way down into the corner of Buck's eye, partly fogging his vision. He wasn't bothered so much by the cut, nor even the rabbit punch old Devil Anse had delivered to his abdomen in a fit of temper, as he was by the cold.

Buck figured from the looks of the misty sun over the tops of the pines that he'd been tied to the tree for about an hour. After punching him up, the two Scraggses—one, he gathered, was the girls' uncle Lyndon Baines—and the two Potters, father and son, had gone down to their pickup trucks to drink beer and talk things over. The more beer the louder the talk. He could hear them distinctly now, discussing profits in the hijack turkey market.

Buck tried his legs experimentally. He could hardly stretch them out, they were so cramped. The Scraggses had him restrained with his own handcuffs, a prime humiliation for any law officer, and his right shoulder and where he was sitting on the half-frozen ground had gone numb.

In a little while the Scraggses and what Devil Anse called the family of the "betrothed"—the Potters, father and son—would come back up to persuade him to adopt their current business agenda. *Lay off investigating Jackson County truck hijackings*, was the message. *Especially turkeys. And lay off the entire spectrum of Scraggs enterprises.*

And oh yes. *Make up his mind about Scarlett.*

They were actually stupid enough to think they'd make him cooperate by beating him up. The jerk in the cowboy hat had been particularly happy to slug him twice in the face while yelling about what he'd probably done to his girl. With, of course, Buck couldn't help thinking, the permission of her grandpa. After they finished this round of beer they'd be back again.

It could go on all afternoon, he thought, checking the slant of the cloud-covered sun. In the meantime, there was the Living Christmas Tree waiting down at the courthouse, and soon, Junior Whitford's committee. And, Buck remembered with a groan, the Atlanta TV cameras. It was too much to hope for a miracle, that the news crews would stay away.

Out of the corner of his eye he was aware of a persistent, slight movement in the trees. Now, as he squinted against the gray light he saw it was the Scraggs dog back there, hiding and watching him.

Fat lot of good the animal had done him. Since it had fallen or been thrown from the truck, he hadn't seen hide nor hair of it. Certainly not while the Scraggses and Potters were beating their current revised business demands into him.

Now that the blood from his cut was no longer seeping into his eye, Buck could see the dog better. The thing knew it, too: it lifted that huge black tail and whacked it in the pine needles several times.

Suddenly inspired, Buck lifted his handcuffed hands and wiggled one finger.

Come closer.

To his surprise the Scraggs dog obeyed, crawling on its belly until it was at the edge of the trees but still in the shade.

Well, that was progress. Hope began to stir, unwillingly. "Go get Farrie," Buck whispered hoarsely.

The dog wagged its tail again.

Damn, it was too much to hope the thing had any sense! He remembered the time when the little sister was hiding, and Scarlett's remark that the dog knew where she was but wouldn't tell. He'd half believed it, then.

"Listen, I need help," Buck rasped. He realized he was pleading with a dumb animal. "Go get help, understand?"

The Scraggs dog wagged its tail again.

Despairing, Buck suddenly had a bright vision of the one good thing he could think of in spite of the Scraggses and in spite of everything. A warm, lovely presence that put its slender arms around him and chased away his misery, his humiliation, the terrible cold.

Scarlett.

"Go," Buck told it, "get Scarlett."

When next he looked, the dog was gone.

Sixteen

SCARLETT HAD NOT ONLY FIXED LUNCH, she'd peeled a bowl of apples and made two apple pies with fancy lattice crusts, but she still felt jittery. Farrie sat at the kitchen table and watched as she started on a package of Betty Crocker brownie mix she'd found in the Grissoms' pantry.

"If you're going to sit around in that Spirit of Mistletoe dress, you're going to have to be careful," Scarlett said as Farrie took the brownie bowl to lick. "It's too late to wash and dry it if you spill something."

Farrie nodded, busy with the chocolate batter. She'd kept her plastic mistletoe headdress on, so ready for her big night that she couldn't bear to take any part of her costume off.

Although they both jumped, it was something of a relief to hear Demon's wild barking, followed by the scratching at the back door. The next instant they knew what it meant.

"Something's happened to Buck," Scarlett cried.

They both raced to open the door. Demon came hurtling in, not stopping to be petted, circling the kitchen table and barking.

"She don't want to stay," Farrie shouted.

Scarlett bent to touch Demon's coat. It was icy cold. "She's been out somewhere with him. I know Demon would never leave Buck unless something's happened!"

Suddenly Scarlett knew what that look meant in Devil Anse's eyes that morning when he'd gotten out of the pickup truck at the Living Christmas Tree. Those eyes that singled her out held a warning not to do anything, no matter what happened.

The dog circled the table again restlessly, still barking her low, rasping *woof, woof.*

Scarlett leaned over it. "Where's *Buck?*" she cried.

Demon barked again and raced for the door. The dog sat down in front of it, tail pounding furiously.

Farrie threw up her hands, her face wrinkled in anguish. "Something's happened for sure, Scarlett!" she screeched. "Is it Devil Anse? Is he going to hurt Sheriff Buck?"

Scarlett's legs gave way under her and she had to sit down. Something awful had happened to Buck. She could guess what that was, since Demon had come back without him.

Oh, glory, she prayed fervently, don't let Devil Anse do anything to Buck! There was no limit to what her grandpa could do, mean as he was!

Scarlett looked slowly around the kitchen. It had all been a dream, she thought. A dream that someone like Farrie and herself could live in a real house, so solid and comfortable, and full of love, like real people. Without being discovered for what they were.

Scraggses. Outlaws. People that no one in their right mind would want to have anything to do with.

What had just happened—what had probably happened to Buck by now if Devil Anse had him— proved that, all right.

She took a deep breath. "We've gotta stop Grandpa," she said, looking across the kitchen table at Farrie. "Buck's been good to us like nobody else has ever been."

She saw her little sister think it over a minute. Then Farrie nodded in agreement.

"And if we do," Scarlett said slowly, "we can never come back."

Farrie's eyes widened. "Whatcha going to do?"

Scarlett shrugged, a little sadly. "I guess you could call it burning our bridges behind us."

This time, they both knew, Devil Anse had gone too far. Sheriff Buck Grissom was different. He was different because Scarlett loved him. And if Devil Anse thought he could do anything he wanted to Buck, he had a big surprise coming.

The bigger surprise the better, Scarlett told herself vengefully. The second mistake Devil Anse had made was thinking she'd forgotten how to act like a Scraggs. Because right now she had just the thing a Scraggs would do in mind.

"If Devil Anse hurts Buck," she vowed as she untied her apron, "I'm going to make him sorry that he ever had any kin at all." She started toward the hallway. "What's in that gun case in the den?"

Her sister was right at her heels. "Two Uzis, an

AK-47," Farrie answered promptly, "and two sawed-off twelve-gauges."

"You've already opened that case to look, haven't you?" Scarlett didn't wait for an answer. "Go pick that lock again," she told her sister, "and get the shotguns."

Unlike most Scraggses Scarlett hated guns. Which didn't keep her from being an unerring shot. She knew Devil Anse wouldn't be so nice-minded when it came to Buck; he'd shoot him dead if he had to.

Well, she could be tough, too, Scarlett thought, when it came to someone she loved. She'd already proved that with Farrie.

She stopped short in front of the den. "Oh, damn, we need a car! What are we going to do for transportation?"

"Mrs. Grissom's Buick Park Avenue?" Farrie looked hopeful. "It's in the garage."

Scarlett turned to her. "What can you do with that?"

"Oh, I love Buicks," Farrie breathed. "I can get in with a coat hanger."

"Then let's do it," Scarlett said.

She gathered up the weapons herself. It took agonizing minutes to find the ammunition for the shotguns, but she finally discovered it in Buck's desk drawer in the den. When she went out to the car Farrie had the Buick's door unlocked and was sprawled on the seat working on the steering column, with only her little feet sticking out from under the long skirt of the Angel's gown.

"You better take off your costume," Scarlett said,

leaning over her to see what she was doing, "and bundle up good. It's getting colder."

Farrie had inserted a screwdriver into the interlocking plastic that covered the steering column. As she pried at it the two sections popped away and fell on the floorboard. She seized the metal rod running up inside the column and pulled on it.

The engine purred into life.

"Push down to shut it off," Farrie said briskly as she sat up. "And pull it up to start. You just don't have any keys, that's all." Her expression changed suddenly as she remembered what Scarlett had said. "I'm not going to take my Spirit of Mistletoe stuff off, Scarlett," she wailed, "I'm going to sing tonight! I just *know* I am!"

"Good night, don't screech." Scarlett stood with one shotgun cradled in one arm, the other shotgun in the other, Farrie's coat in her hand. "I only said that because I just don't know if we're going to get back in time."

"Yes we are! Demon's a good tracker, Scarlett," she pleaded. "We just have to follow behind her and hope we don't get into too much traffic. If we do, you can get out and go with her," she cried, her voice rising again. "I can drive the Buick, you *know* I can!"

"Now, now," Scarlett soothed her. She handed Farrie her cap, mittens, and down jacket. Her little sister had been driving since she was eight, but her feet didn't quite reach the pedals.

"Well, we'll see," Scarlett said, as she got in behind the Buick's wheel. Demon was already in the driveway, tail wagging impatiently. Scarlett set her jaw.

"I hope," she said under her breath as she drove the Buick out of the garage, "you haven't done anything to Buck, Devil Anse, I really do. 'Cause if you have, I'll sure make you pay for it."

A steady north wind bent the tops of the pine trees in the gully. It didn't reach where Buck was sitting on the ground, tied to his pine, but another hour, he knew, and he was going to feel more than his numbing backside.

He'd been watching the men down where the pickups were parked. There'd been another round of beer and discussion, with the Scraggs uncle and the Potters turning to look at him from time to time. Only old Devil Anse kept his back turned.

Well, he sure as hell wasn't giving them what they wanted, which was to have the Jackson County sheriff in their pocket so they'd have a free hand, even outright protection if that's what it came down to, from the county police for what old Scraggs called their "business interests." And if bribery failed, they planned to beat him until he gave in. Buck knew they were ready to come back and persuade him some more.

He looked up through the pines above him. The winter sun was in a bank of gray clouds and twilight was reaching into the gully. The hell of it was if they beat him into unconsciousness it wouldn't do them any good, he was damned if he was going to give in to an old thug like Devil Anse. And in spite of the fact that the Living Christmas Tree was due to start after dusk with Junior Whitford, and the Atlanta television news.

I'm going to be an item in the media, he thought, one way or the other. Right now I think it's going to be more like: "Jackson County's Sheriff Mysteriously Missing When All Hell Breaks Loose at the Courthouse."

And all hell *would* break loose when it was discovered that he'd spent the afternoon tied to a tree, being beaten by redneck hijackers, rather than policing the Living Christmas Tree concert. He might as well resign, Buck told himself. It was better than waiting to be kicked out of office.

He turned his face up to the sky and the soughing pine branches, and shut his eyes and said a small prayer.

Scarlett, he prayed silently, I sent your damned monster animal to you, and I hope you've contacted the department by now and have my deputies on their way while there's still time. If you haven't—

He couldn't go any further. Loud redneck voices interrupted. When he opened his eyes he saw the Scraggses and the Potters toss their beer cans into the trees and start up toward him.

At the junction of Route 19 and the feeder road leading to State 135 Demon stopped, confused, on the shoulder.

Scarlett slammed on the Buick's brakes. Traffic was heavy with tractor-trailer rigs barreling down the slopes of the Blue Ridge from North Carolina. She saw Demon waver, then start to cross the road.

"Scarlett!" Farrie screamed.

Scarlett cut a sharp U-turn against traffic as an eighteen-wheeler bore down on them, horn blaring. She didn't know whether they'd lost Demon or not until they turned onto the side road and could see her. But the dog had slowed. Not only slowed, she was limping.

Scarlett groaned.

"Now you get to drive," she told Farrie as she pulled the Buick to the side of the road and got out. "From here on I'm going to have to follow Demon on foot. You keep a good ways behind us, and do what I say, Farrie, or I'll take a stick to you!"

Scarlett never threatened her sister, but neither could they afford to let Demon get run over. Her mouth open in surprise, Farrie nodded.

Several cars sped by. Scarlett took Demon by the collar. The dog pulled against her, whimpering, dragging her along.

As they started down the road Demon finally broke free and ran ahead. At the curve, Scarlett stopped and shaded her eyes. It seemed as though she could see the baby-blue paint of a customized pickup through the pine trees.

Farrie pulled the Buick up behind her and stuck her head out the window. "Is it them?" she cried, excited. "Can you see Sheriff Buck?"

Scarlett put her finger to her lips. It would be like Devil Anse and the Potters to take Buck out into the woods. It all depended now on what they'd been doing to him, as to what she was going to do to *them*.

Working quietly, Scarlett got the shotguns and the shells out of the trunk and gave Farrie one.

"Don't do anything now, without I tell you to," she warned. "I'm not fool enough to give you an unloaded gun so's somebody can kill you, but that don't mean I want you to kill somebody, either."

They scrambled down into the gully that ran at a right angle to the road. Just when they thought they could hear voices ahead, a figure in a gray business suit popped up out of a tangle of persimmon bushes and creepers, right on top of them, nearly scaring them to death.

Scarlett jerked up the weapon she was carrying. Farrie choked back a scream.

"Wait!" the figure said.

It was too late. Demon had already launched herself into the air. She hit the Scraggses' lookout and bore him to the ground.

As Demon stood on the man's chest, his voice and breath blown out of him, Scarlett looked down into a totally strange face. But there was no time to ask questions. "Keep your mouth shut," she hissed. "Or I'll blow your head off."

She left Farrie standing over the lookout with the shotgun pointed at his head, and lunged downward on the pine slopes, Demon following.

The gully ended and here the woods were more open. Scarlett stood hidden in some persimmon bushes where she could see Buck Grissom tied to a tree. Devil Anse and Loy Potter, Reese's father, were punching him. All Scarlett could see was blood. After one particularly vicious blow, she heard him groan.

They were hurting Buck!

A sob tore out of Scarlett. Not a very Scraggs

thing to do, but she couldn't help it. Outrage propelled her out of the bushes, shotgun in hand.

"You get your hands off him!" The shriek burst out of her with a blast from the gun that sprayed into the dirt. "Oh, look at that blood!" she screeched. "You've busted his poor nose again!"

There was a moment's silence as the men turned. Then a look of disbelief followed quickly by expressions of horror.

"Great God, it's Scarlett!" her uncle Lyndon Baines shouted. "That girl doesn't stop at nothin'!"

With a scream, Loy Potter made a running jump into the gully, followed by his son. Devil Anse stood where he was.

"Scarlett, honey—" he whined.

"Don't call me honey, you old fiend!" Furious, tears running down her face, Scarlett lifted the 12 gauge and shot up the top of the pine tree Buck was tied to. Green needles showered down around them.

There were hoarse screams from the gully. "Run, Anse, she'll shoot you, too!" the unseen voice that was her uncle Lyndon Baines yelled again. "You know how Scarlett is!"

Scarlett turned the shotgun in that direction and fired again. The two Potters hurtled out of the end of the gully and ran for their truck, her uncle Lyndon Baines not far behind.

Scarlett turned back to Devil Anse. "Give me the gun, Scarlett, honey," he was wheedling.

"Demon, go get him!" Scarlett ordered. With a roar the dog threw itself on the old outlaw and bore him to the ground.

That done, Scarlett raced for Buck. She was weeping outright as she fell to her knees. "Oh, my darling love." Gently, she touched his bloody face with her fingertips. "I can never make it up to you for what my kinfolk have done. I'm gonna let Demon chew Grandpa to rotten little pieces for doing this to you," she vowed. Hiccoughs replaced the sobs as she bent to peer at him. "Oh lordy, now you really are going to have to get your nose fixed!"

"Scarlett," Buck said indistinctly. He'd found what seemed to be a loose tooth. "Don't do anything. Just get your little sister to come pick the lock and get me out of these handcuffs. Quick."

"Right away, hon," Scarlett whispered. She couldn't help it, she bent over him and touched his mouth, his forehead with feather-light kisses. "Oh, I love you so much," she moaned. "It's all ruined now, I guess. But I wish you just loved me, too, even if I am a Scraggs."

"I love you, Scarlett," Buck said truthfully, "being a Scraggs has nothing to do with it. And we're going to get married, too. But right now if we don't get back to town and the Living Christmas Tree program, I'm going to lose my job."

"You love me?" she whispered, her eyes like stars. "You really *love* me? Do you know what you just said?"

Buck tried to raise himself up, a difficult move because of his shoulder. "Is the dog killing Devil Anse?" he wanted to know.

Gently, Scarlett put both hands on the sides of his face. "No, it just *sounds* like Demon's tearing his throat out. That's just so he won't try to get away."

"Scarlett," Buck said again, urgently.

"Yes, love," she murmured, still gazing at him with adoration in her eyes. "Farrie'll come and pick the lock on your handcuffs and we'll get you out of here. Right after she ties up the lookout."

"Lookout?" Buck said. "What lookout?"

A few minutes later Buck lifted Byron Turnipseed from the ground as best he could using his disabled arm, and set him on his feet.

"I'm sure sorry about this," Buck said. "What we had was—ah, a case of mistaken identity. The dog had you tagged as the hijackers' lookout."

"Oh, not at all, Sheriff, not at all." The Georgia criminal investigation department officer bent over to pick up his glasses and his gray fedora. "I should have let you know I was in the vicinity. That was tremendous K-Nine work, I didn't even know you were training dogs up here in Jackson County. Your animal took me out very efficiently, without a scratch." He examined the elbow of his gray suit, which was missing. "Well, my clothes sustained a little damage, but nothing to worry about." He looked around, nodding approvingly. "Yes, really a commendable piece of work, your K-Nine holding me down like that until the handler took over."

"I'm not the handler," Farrie piped, "I'm a—"

"*Witness*," Buck said loudly. He pushed Farrie, who was still carrying her sawed-off shotgun, behind him while his face told Scarlett to do something with her little sister. "It's a little unusual using a juvenile, but it—ah, cracked the case."

"No it didn't," Farrie shouted, "*Scarlett* did! Y'all

aren't listening to me, but I gotta get outta here. They're already starting down at the courthouse!"

"And I'm glad to see you've got women on the force now," Turnipseed said, turning to Scarlett. "Undercover, too. That's fine affirmative action, Buck, considering the limited size of your department."

"The child's got a point, it's getting late." Buck tactfully herded them toward the Blazer, keeping the shotgun pointed at Devil Anse's neck. "I believe I told you about the trouble with the injunction against religious scenes on courthouse property."

"As a matter of fact," the CID man responded, "I saw it on television."

"Yes, well." Buck looked around, giving himself a moment to think. "It looks like I'm going to have to move this prisoner with us. I'll tell you the details in a minute."

He wished he knew the details himself. His deputies were expecting him in town at any time. Yet if he followed procedure, he had to deliver Devil Anse to the jail and book him, and send out an APB for the uncle and the two Potters. At any other time Buck could have radioed for a deputy to come to his assistance, but nearly the entire sheriff's department, most of them on overtime, were downtown.

He saw Farrie climbing into what he recognized as his mother's Buick. "Scarlett," she was shrilling, "I need my mistletoe crown! Where'd you put it?"

Beside Buck, Devil Anse said something evil under his breath. Buck speeded up the old man's progress by jamming the shotgun a little more firmly under his ear. Whatever happened, Buck had to get to the courthouse before the television people arrived, and the Hare Krishnas. Not to mention Junior and his committee.

Scarlett was practically running to keep up with them. "Buck, listen," she said, "I can take Grandpa—"

He shook his head.

Buck knew he virtually owed his life to her. She was worried about being a Scraggs, but Scarlett was the finest, most courageous woman he had ever known. He'd never forget the sight of her spraying the trees with the shotgun, driving off the Potters and the uncle, and rescuing him. Besides that, he thought, looking down at her, she was beautiful. She made his heart pound just being near her.

No matter what she said Buck couldn't take a chance and trust the old scoundrel with her. Or Byron Turnipseed, for that matter. Handcuffed and with the barrel of the shotgun to his head, Ancil Scraggs looked quiet enough, but that didn't mean he wouldn't try to take advantage of someone to escape.

Below, they heard Farrie screeching about getting to the Living Christmas Tree in time for her solo. The kid was right; they couldn't afford to delay one moment longer.

But what the hell was he going to do with Devil Anse?

"Leave the cars here," Buck ordered as they reached the road. "We'll go in the county vehicle."

Byron Turnipseed, Farrie, and the Scraggs dog piled into the Blazer's back seat among Kevin Black Badger's camping gear. There wasn't much room.

Scarlett watched them, biting her lip. Then she suddenly took Buck's arm and pulled him aside.

"Not now, sweetheart," Buck said, jabbing Devil Anse in the ribs to urge him into the front passenger's side, "we're in a hell of a hurry."

But when he turned to look at her he saw the cold had made her cheeks the color of mountain apples, and the wind was playfully tangling her black hair. She was so lovely he couldn't drag his eyes away.

"You gotta do something about my grandpa, don't you?" she asked.

Devil Anse quickly leaned out of the Blazer. "Scarlett, honey," he rasped, "you listen to your old granddaddy a minute. If it's love and ro-mance you want, sugar, I can find you somebody better than this lop-eared, retard excuse for a sheriff, who only got his job because of his pa. Now—"

"You shut up," Scarlett said. She kept her eyes on Buck's battered face. "Buck, I—you want to listen," she said, "because I have an idea."

They couldn't stand there all day. But Buck couldn't stop watching her dimples, that lovely mouth. "Go right ahead, sweetheart," he said huskily, "if you've got an idea, let's have it."

After all, he told himself, whatever she had in mind, it couldn't make things much worse than they were.

Seventeen

BYRON TURNIPSEED WRAPPED ONE OF Kevin Black Badger's camp blankets around him and drew it over his head with some difficulty, as he was crowded on one side by Farrie and Demon, and on the other by Scarlett, who was holding the shotgun to the back of Devil Anse's head as he rode in front with Buck.

"There now," the state CID man said, his eyeglasses twinkling in the rapidly deepening dusk, "think I'll pass as a shepherd?"

Farrie regarded him solemnly. "You need another piece of rope for your head. That's the way shepherds look on TV."

"Absolutely right," he agreed. He reached into the back of the Blazer where Scarlett had cut several small lengths of Black Badger's tent cord and selected a piece. He wrapped it around his head to hold the blanket in place, Middle Eastern-style.

"I have to tell you, Sheriff," Turnipseed said, raising his voice as the Blazer turned off the highway and careened onto Main Street and headed for the courthouse, "I never expected to find such innovative law-enforcement procedures up here. But I'm really impressed. In my experience and, I might say, most of us in the state CID, the majority of your little mountain counties up here seem unable to approach law-enforcement work with any—uh, creativity."

"Oh, we're creative, all right," Buck said grimly. He shot a glance at Devil Anse, also wrapped vaguely Arabian-style in a camp blanket. "I only hope this damned thing works."

Farrie bounced up and down in her seat in suppressed excitement. She'd watched, big-eyed, as Scarlett had put a piece of paper towel in Devil Anse's mouth, tied it in place with Kevin Black Badger's bandana, then pulled the blanket around him. "Oh, it will work, Buck," she squeaked, "I know it will! Tonight nothing's going to go wrong!"

Buck knew all too well that plenty could still go wrong. It was a good thing Byron Turnipseed had agreed to do what he was doing and give them enough time to go first to the courthouse with their prisoner. Otherwise there wouldn't have been any plan at all.

"Demon looks nice, too." Farrie looked fondly at the big dog beside her, who promptly snaked out a gigantic red tongue to lick her face. "It's not just any dog," she said proudly, "that'd let you wrap it up in somebody's sheepskin. Now you got to be careful," she told the animal, "and not let it fall off, y'hear? You're supposed to be a shepherd's sheep."

The courthouse was in sight. Buck stepped on the

gas in spite of the fact that the area was filled with large crowds and a number of illegally parked vehicles, including not one but several TV news vans. Buck swore when he saw a television van from a station in Chattanooga.

He turned the Blazer down a side street, looking for a parking space. The Living Christmas Tree was already singing. They could hear the faint refrain of "Deck the Halls" wafting toward them on the cold night air.

Farrie heard it, too. "Scarlett," she shrieked. "You gotta let me out!"

"Well," Buck said, raising his voice, "we're not making a direct reference to religion with two shepherds and a dog playing a sheep. That could be anything. But on the other hand somebody might pick up on it."

There was a chorus of protests behind him.

"Nonsense, shepherds and sheep are as innocuous as Christmas angels, reindeer, and—uh, elves," Byron Turnipseed said.

"We can't stop now," Scarlett cried. "Not after all this."

"Well," Buck responded doggedly, "I still think it would be better if I let Byron hang around the back of the crowd discreetly keeping the drop on Scraggs with the shotgun."

"Holding a gun on Scraggs out in the open?" the CID man said. "Now *that* would really attract attention!" Surprisingly, he chuckled. "Myself, I've always liked the wonderful spy-story twists where if you want to hide something, you put it right out where everybody can see it. This one's a classic."

"It won't be but for a few minutes, anyway," Scarlett put in. "Just as long as it takes for Buck to help me get Farrie up in the tree."

"Now they're singing again!" Farrie screamed. Demon, the sheepskin wobbling precariously, joined her with deep barks. Farrie clawed at the Blazer's door. "Oh, Scarlett, I'm going to miss my solo!"

Buck bellowed, "Stay where you are!" Nevertheless, he shot the Blazer into the only space available between two television news vans.

At that moment, to the stunned amazement of everyone inside the van except Devil Anse, who was trying to dislodge his gag, the air was ripped by a series of explosions. This was followed by tremendous flashes of green, red, yellow, and white that lit up the sky. Farrie, her mouth open, couldn't even scream.

"They went ahead and did it," Buck sputtered, getting out and opening the door. "Fireworks! The city council and their damned fireworks! That's all we need!"

All around them crowds massed in the square and over the courthouse lawn ooh'd and aah'd as the next brilliant concussion shook the skies. Buck looked around, but none of his deputies was in sight.

"Stay together," he shouted as they hurried toward the Christmas tree.

"Sheriff?" A figure loomed in front of him, carrying a TV camera on its shoulder. "You are the Jackson County sheriff, aren't you? Are you expecting a demonstration here tonight by the—"

"Out of my way," Buck snarled, pushing past him.

Whoooooouum, roared a rocket. Closely followed by the *BLAM* of a hundred tiny golden fish wriggling across the night sky. Several babies in the crowd started to cry.

"Not bad, not bad," Byron Turnipseed shouted as he stumbled along in his blanket behind Buck, who held the shotgun firmly but unobtrusively pressed to the small of Devil Anse's back. "You've got to admit the noise of the fireworks is great cover. Hitchcock himself couldn't have done any better!"

As they approached the tree a figure dashed up to them and grabbed Farrie's arm. "Where have you been? You've given me a nervous breakdown, kid," the band teacher screamed over the mind-altering explosions of several percussive rockets overhead. "We've already started! How're you going to get up in the tree now?" he demanded at the top of his lungs.

Farrie looked at Buck, her lip quivering. Her hand in his tightened. She said, so low he could hardly hear her, "I don't climb so good."

Scarlett said, "Farrie, you don't—"

"Wait a minute!" Buck bent over and looked down into the pinched little face. For a moment the fireworks were so noisy he couldn't speak. Then he said loudly to Farrie, "Don't worry about a thing, babe. I'll get you up in the Living Christmas Tree before I do anything else."

He took her hand again. "I'll take Farrie up," he told the music teacher. Their faces turned green and red in a shower of rocket light. "Just make sure somebody's waiting for her when she gets up there."

Another television cameraman hurried up followed by a young woman with a script in her hand. The TV newswoman promptly stepped beside Buck and Farrie and said to the bank of portable lights the technician turned on, "This is Jennifer James live from Nancyville, Georgia, with some of the performers in the town's controversial Living Christmas Tree."

"He's not a performer," Mr. Ravenwood yelled, pushing her out of the way, "he's the *sheriff!*"

"Are you *really* the Jackson County sheriff?" Jennifer James followed them, microphone extended. "Your face seems rather battered, Sheriff. Is this the result of some violence that has already taken place because of the controversy up here?"

Buck pushed the mike away, shaking his head. "C'mon, kid," he said to Farrie. He took her hand and started for the back of the Living Christmas Tree. He had already seen the blanketed figures of Byron Turnipseed and Devil Anse and a hybrid fleecy-canine figure take a position down front. Thank goodness they seemed to be in semidarkness.

At the foot of the tree's ladderlike stairs, Farrie pulled back, screaming every time a rocket went off.

Scarlett tried to soothe her. "We never seen fireworks but once," she yelled. "I don't think she was big enough to remember."

"I don't wanna go up there," Farrie screamed, "they'll hit me!"

It wasn't just the fireworks, Buck knew. He remembered the desolate look in those black eyes when she'd whispered to him she didn't climb so good.

And didn't walk too good, he told himself. *And all the other things, including being a Scraggs.*

He lifted Farrie in his arms, wincing with the stab of pain in his shoulder. "Farrie?" He knew she heard because she gulped, then shuddered. "You've done nothing but yell the past hour about how much you wanted to get here. Now," Buck said, his mouth at her ear, "I want you to go up there and sing. You can sing better than anybody else and you know it. Let's see you *do* it!"

The little pixie face lifted to him, tear-stained and surprised. She said something, but fireworks noise drowned it out.

"Sing!" Buck told her. "I know you can do it, kid. Just stop bawling."

Farrie's arms went around his neck suddenly and she clung to him. Finally she nodded. In spite of himself, Buck smiled.

"You take me," he heard her say. "Only you!"

"You got it," he assured her.

They went up the first stairs into the tree and hands reached out to them. "Go get 'em, Farrie," the Bells yelled over the thunder of rockets.

"I'll take her," Judy Heamstead said when they reached the Angels. "It's only a few steps more."

Buck shook his head. He needed to be down on the courthouse grounds, but, like his dad, he never broke his word. "I told her I'd carry her all the way. Wouldn't let her down now. That right, kid?"

Eyes shining, Farrie grinned at him.

Two men in the robes of the Presbyterian church choir were waiting on the last level. They reached out and took her from Buck's arms. "Glad to see you got here," one of them said as he set Farrie on her feet. "You ready to sing, honey?"

Farrie was telling them she was when Buck turned to go. He was looking forward to hustling Byron Turnipseed, old man Scraggs, and the dog to a safer, less public place. He was on the tree's bottom level when a roar from hundreds of throats went up, then he heard the unmistakable sound of a plane swooping low.

"Santa Claus," the crowd was yelling.

Buck jumped the remaining feet to the ground. The plane, with a big Night Sun spotlight playing over the courthouse lawn, was getting ready to release the city council's freebie Santa.

Buck struggled to get through what seemed like a wall of bodies with faces all turned to the sky. The fireworks were over, but their problems weren't. The courthouse environs were no shopping mall parking lot; a jump there was hazardous, as any fool should know. Especially after dark.

Deputy Kevin Black Badger materialized at Buck's elbow, dark circles under his eyes. "Sheriff," Kevin said belligerently, planting himself so Buck could not pass him, "is that a dog over there by the tree wearing my best imported Australian sheepskin rug that was in my camping equipment?" He stopped, abruptly, to peer into Buck's face. "Good Lord, who beat you up?"

"Later," Buck told him brusquely.

A cheer had gone up as Santa, carrying a big black bag, jumped out of the low-flying Cessna and did a lengthy free-fall before opening his parachute.

Buck swore under his breath. "Go get the ambulance and fire rescue on the radio," he told Black Badger.

The deputy looked up and calculated the drift of Santa's chute over them. "Yes, *sir!*" Black Badger left at a run.

The circling plane's searchlight, sweeping over the crowd, now picked out what seemed to be a budget version of two shepherds and a strangely extraterrestrial sheep, the latter now snarling viciously at one of the shepherds.

Another roar went up as the light illuminated the trio. People stood up and pointed. One shepherd hitched closer to the crowd as if trying to disappear into it. The sheep promptly dragged him back, teeth clamped in his robes.

A voice in the crowd cried, "Sheep and shepherds? Are we going to have the manger scene after all?"

There was a ragged cheer.

Buck had spotted a familiar figure. "Mose," he shouted to his deputy. The noise was too great; Mose hadn't heard him. Beyond Mose a line of men and women approached from the courthouse parking lot carrying signs that read: RESTORE THE REAL MEANING OF CHRISTMAS, NO SEPARATION OF CHURCH AND STATE, and ABANDON PAGANISM NOW!

But no Holy Family, Buck saw, straining his eyes to read the placards. Maybe Junior had given them a fighting chance after all.

He got halfway across the lawn before he tripped over a stroller and almost fell on familiar saffron-robed figures. The Hare Krishnas, too, were seemingly headed in the direction of Junior's committee.

As Buck staggered to his feet the nearest one chanted *hare ram* at him quite hostilely, and pushed him away.

Buck pried the stroller loose from his leg as the viewers around him yelled for him to get down, they couldn't see Santa Claus. But above them Santa was having his own troubles as he drifted inexorably toward the courthouse trees.

"Go on, go on!" In front of the Living Christmas Tree, Mr. Ravenwood, arms lifted, was shouting to his chorus, "Don't look at the *plane*, look at me! Let's have the last number!"

While most of the crowd watched, enthralled, Santa Claus floated into one of the oldest oak trees on the courthouse property, struck, and hung there, swinging gently. His black Christmas bag dropped to the ground. As one, the crowd groaned.

At that moment the Living Christmas Tree struck up their rendition of "I Saw Mommy Kissing Santa Claus." The sign-carrying group of the Committee for the Real Meaning of Christmas had reached the shepherd and sheep tableau at the foot of the Christmas tree. Before they could plant their signs, there were the distinct sounds of snarls and growls, followed by loud screams. Those who were not watching the dangling Santa in the oak tree were treated to the spectacle of Junior's militant committee members throwing their signs away and scattering, apparently pursued by a vicious, slavering sheep.

Television reporters promptly raced past Buck to cover the Real Meaning of Christmas Committee being assaulted at the foot of the Living Christmas

Tree. In the distance the howl of sirens forecast the arrival of the Nancyville fire rescue unit.

"Scarlett!" Buck shouted. He couldn't find her anywhere. He hoped to hell she wasn't caught in the melee down by Devil Anse and the CID man.

He finally reached Moses Holt at the jam-packed courthouse steps. In a few seconds, with Mose's walkie-talkie in hand, Buck had rounded up his deputies and assigned them to crowd, television crew, and Santa-hanging-in-the-tree control. He saw Kevin Black Badger had already separated Junior's committee from the perils of a maddened sheep and a shepherd apparently trying to tear off his robes hampered by a pair of handcuffs. The fire rescue was moving to put a ladder under the gently swinging figure of Santa Claus.

Scarlett, he thought. Where the devil was she?

Suddenly it began to snow.

No one noticed it at first, there was too much happening all at once. But thick, white, starry shapes began falling rapidly out of a dark sky, swirling gently over Nancyville's valley.

As the snowfall became noticeable the crowd quieted somewhat. Translucent clouds of snow, hushed and peaceful, drifted down on the courthouse lawn, the singers assembled in the wooden Living Christmas Tree, on the deputies moving the Hare Krishnas to a quieter place.

Scarlett, standing under the wooden struts of the Living Christmas Tree, looked up and saw Farrie move forward, answering Mr. Ravenwood's hoarse call.

At the same time, Buck was at the back of the

crowd. *"Brrraarckkk, Sheriff?"* the radio in his hand said. "Are you there?" But Buck stood unmoving, not answering, as the flashlight "candles" on the tree came on. The structure rapidly blossomed with lights, gently veiled in the snow, illuminating "Bells" and the "Angels." Who had their eyes on Cyrus Ravenwood, waiting for their cues.

A murmuring silence settled over the crowd except for a few small babies wailing and the subdued noises from the fire rescue team hauling a precautionary stretcher up into the oak tree.

Gradually the snowy night, the silence of the mountains around them settled on the crowd as the words of the last Christmas song began. Farrie Scraggs's big, unchildlike voice drifted out from the top of the tree.

> "I heard the bells on Christmas Day,
> Their old familiar carols play,
> And wild and sweet, the words repeat—"

Fifty-odd voices on the tree joined in: *"Of peace on earth, Goodwill to men!"*

During the chorus Buck managed to catch Kevin Black Badger's eye and signal that he wanted him. His deputy started through the crowd.

Farrie took the solo again:

> "And in despair, I bowed my head
> There is no peace on earth, I said,
> For hate is strong, and mocks the song—"

Now some in the crowd were singing. *"Of peace on earth, Goodwill to men!"*

Scarlett was helping Byron Turnipseed haul Devil Anse to his feet when Buck and Kevin Black Badger appeared.

"That's about it," Buck whispered, as the deputy took the shotgun from the CID man's hands and marched Ancil Scraggs away. Byron Turnipseed was beaming behind his glasses.

"Wonderful operation, Sheriff," he said, pumping Buck's hand. "You set a bang-up example up here! I'm going to write this up, not just for state law-enforcement publications, but national, too."

Above them Farrie's voice floated out over the dark air. In the crowd, many people had suddenly joined hands.

"Then pealed the bells, more loud and deep—"

On cue, all the church bells in Nancyville began to ring: a deep *bong, bong* from the bell towers of the Presbyterians, Methodists, and Baptists, a higher, rapid clanging from the carillons of Episcopal St. George's. Farrie sang:

"That wrong shall fail, the right prevail—"

Longfellow's message, not just a song now, spoke to all those listening. There was not a sound as faces turned up to the singer. Then, as the bells from the valley's churches grew louder some people in the crowd got to their feet.

"Of peace on earth," the voices of the chorus pro-
claimed. *"Goodwill to men!"*

The crowd around the courthouse was singing,
including Junior's committee and the fire rescue
team, who had paused in their efforts in the oak tree
to join in.

Church bells clanged and vibrated exultantly on
the night air. Above them rose Farrie's powerful
contralto voice.

> *"Till ringing, singing on its way,*
> The world revolved from night to day
> A voice, a chime, a chant sublime—"

Suddenly, as if there had been some agreement
beforehand that everyone on the courthouse lawn
would stand up and join in the chorus, a thousand
voices sent a triumphant refrain floating up into the
falling snow and the heavens above it:

> *"Of peace on earth, Goodwill to men!"*

No one did anything for several long minutes.
Some people turned and hugged each other.
Hugged total strangers. One by one in the thickly
falling snow the audience folded up their chairs and
blankets and made for their cars, their smiles and
subdued voices held by the magic of the song. Santa
Claus, removed from the tree, showed his gratitude
to the members of the fire rescue team by hugging
them, tearfully.

Judy and one of the Bells helped Farrie down and she threw herself upon Scarlett, burying her face.

"You did good, hon," Scarlett told her, stroking her hair. "It was beautiful."

Eighteen

"YOU NEED TO DROP BY THE HOSPITAL, Sheriff," Kevin Black Badger said, "and see about your face. Your right eye is just about shut."

Buck only grunted.

He knew what he was going to do about his face. Just as soon as he could get away from the nearly deserted courthouse area, he had plans to go home with Scarlett and sit before the Christmas tree in the parlor, listening to Christmas music, while she treated the eye, his cut lip, and various bruises with ice-cold compresses.

It was not exactly the most romantic evening with someone you loved, but Buck couldn't wait to get started.

"Devil Anse?" he asked Black Badger. Buck's upper lip was swelling, putting a limit on conversation.

"All booked and processed," Kevin told him, "and in a cell down at the jail." The deputy hesitated, seeing Scarlett coming across the littered lawn with Farrie. "I—ah, well, Sheriff, I want to say I don't have no hard feelings about you using my stuff to-night," he said, his eyes on her. "I think I can salvage what's left of my sheepskin. Make car seats out of it, maybe."

"Good idea." Buck watched the deputy turn and abruptly walk away, the Scraggs dog at his heels. He started to call out to Black Badger, then thought better of it. It looked as though the animal was going to follow the deputy all the way to his patrol car.

Then, suddenly, there was Scarlett.

Even Buck's swollen eye managed to open a little more at the sight of her. She was so beautiful bundled in an old down ski coat from the church boxes, flushed with the cold, snowflakes in her night-dark hair.

She slipped her cold hand in his.

"You all right?" he said huskily.

She nodded, her eyes like black stars. "You were good to Farrie. I want to thank you."

"No more than what I should have done." Buck turned to look at the imp beside him. "You better go get your dog," he told her. "I don't know what got into it, going off with Black Badger. But right now it looks like the thing's trying to get into his patrol car."

Farrie viewed the deputy struggling with the huge dog for a long moment, then she shrugged. "She'll do that sometimes," she said calmly. "I dunno—maybe Demon thinks he needs something."

Kevin Black Badger *needed* something? Buck turned to Scarlett, but she only hugged his arm with both hands and said, "Maybe your deputy's lonely."

Buck was damned if he could follow this. But if they weren't worried about the dog, he surely wasn't. "She'll come back," Farrie put in consolingly, "she always does. Demon does what she wants to."

He'd already learned that. Buck took Scarlett's hand and tucked it under his arm and they began walking toward the Blazer.

While they were sitting before the Christmas tree at home and she was putting ice on his face, Buck planned to have a talk with Scarlett about the future. He'd never intended to live with his mother forever. In fact, he'd hired an architect some years ago to draw up plans for an A-frame he'd like to build up on Makim's Mountain.

Farrie hurried to keep up with them. Just as they approached the courthouse parking lot, empty now except for one snow-covered television van, a somewhat bedraggled female figure came limping toward them.

"Oh, Sheriff!" The TV camera on the shoulder of the cameraman following her began to roll. "It's Jennifer James. I'm so glad I found you! Do you have anything you want to say about the—ah, dramatic and controversial events that took place here in Nancyville tonight?"

Scarlett tried to pull away, but Buck held her firmly. It was all over, there was nothing to get upset about. In fact, if anything, it had all turned out pretty well. He grabbed Farrie with his free hand and turned them both to face the camera.

"Yeah, as a matter of fact, I do," Buck said, mindful of his split lip and the need to keep it short. "I hope you got all of us singing 'Peace on earth,

213

goodwill to men,' because that's the message from mountain people up here to the world. And it's a good one. We hope the world pays attention."

He put his arms around Scarlett and drew her to him, hoping that his pride and love showed on what was left of his face.

"I'd like," he said, "to announce that I'm getting married to Miss Scarlett Scraggs of the—ah, prominent Scraggs family of this area. Her sister, Miss Farrah Fawcett Scraggs, will be her bridesmaid."

He heard Farrie gasp. Scarlett pulled back to stare at him.

"Wish us luck," Buck said, hurrying Scarlett and her sister away before they could say anything.

But Scarlett stopped short and wrenched her arm away to yell, "We're *engaged?* We really are? Like we're going to get *married?* You must mean it! You just told everybody that on *television!*"

"We have to talk about it later," Buck told her. "But engaged, married, yeah." If it hadn't been for his lip, he would have grinned.

"You told the whole world that you're going to marry a *Scraggs?*" Scarlett flung herself on him, making Buck stagger back a few steps, and threw her arms around his neck. "Oh, Buck Grissom, you are the kindest, bravest—"

"Nice to kids, too," Farrie yelled, inching up to try to put her arms around both of them.

"—most loving man," Scarlett breathed, looking up into Buck's eyes. "I could just kiss you!"

"Wait just a few minutes, sweetheart," Buck said, pulling her arms from around his neck. "You can kiss me all you want when we get home."

"Home." Farrie hobbled after them, looking excited. "Scarlett, ask him if—"

But the newswoman was coming after them. "Sheriff, just a minute. That's very interesting, what you said about getting married. Can we ask you a few more—"

Buck seized both Scraggs sisters by the hand and loped toward the Blazer. He couldn't wait a minute longer. His face hurt like hell, but if he was careful he might be able to hold Scarlett Scraggs in his arms and get in the kisses she wanted there before the Christmas tree.

"We need to make some plans, Scarlett," he said, as he opened the Blazer door for her. "Like how many kids we're going to have, where to build a house, that sort of thing."

She looked at him, eyes wide. "Actually, I was thinking I'd like to open a restaurant."

Restaurant? Buck thought that over as he lifted Farrie into the back.

"They told me," Farrie was saying happily, "and Mr. Ravenwood the music teacher did, too, that I could be a country and western singer like Reba McEntire and Patsy Cline." She looked at him with adoration in her eyes. "But you know, I think now I'd rather be a *cop!*"

"Law-enforcement officer," Buck said automatically.

He sighed as he slid behind the wheel. *Restaurant.* He supposed he could live with that. And the pixie child wanted to be a deputy. That was going to be a little tougher.

Somehow, Buck found, looking around, he

missed the damned dog. *She'll be back*, Farrie had said. Buck couldn't help it, he shuddered.

"Oh, look at it snow!" Scarlett cuddled close to him in the front seat, her warm mouth at his ear. Buck put his arm around her. In the Blazer's back seat, Farrie was singing softly to herself.

"We never had a Christmas like this one," Scarlett whispered happily.

Buck recklessly leaned over, considering that he was driving with only one arm, to kiss the top of her beautiful head. He could just about gauge the reaction in Nancyville—in all of north Georgia—when their engagement announcement showed up on the television evening news. But Nancyville would just have to get used to it, he told himself. As far as he was concerned, the Scraggses were there to stay.

"Neither," Sheriff Buck told his fiancée with great satisfaction as they turned into the road to the mountain, "have I."